By JOHN TERRY MOORE

Black Dog
The Eleventh Commandment
A Nice Normal Family

Published by DREAMSPINNER PRESS
www.dreamspinnerpress.com

The
Eleventh
Commandment

John Terry Moore

Published by
DREAMSPINNER PRESS

5032 Capital Circle SW, Suite 2, PMB# 279,
Tallahassee, FL 32305-7886 USA
www.dreamspinnerpress.com

This is a work of fiction. Names, characters, places, and incidents either
are the product of author imagination or are used fictitiously, and any
resemblance to actual persons, living or dead, business establishments,
events, or locales is entirely coincidental.

The Eleventh Commandment
© 2021 John Terry Moore

Cover Art
© 2021 Maria Fanning
Cover content is for illustrative purposes only and any person depicted
on the cover is a model.

Mass Market Paperback ISBN: 978-1-64108-266-2
Trade Paperback ISBN: 978-1-64405-885-5
Digital ISBN: 978-1-64405-884-8
Mass Market published April 2022
v. 1.0

Printed in the United States of America
∞
This paper meets the requirements of
ANSI/NISO Z39.48-1992 (Permanence of Paper).

To my husband, Russell

Acknowledgments

PHYLLIS CLARKE and Martin Griffin for their assistance in launching *Black Dog* and *A Nice Normal Family*.

Author's Note

I APOLOGIZE in advance to those who feel righteously offended, once again, with me taking the piss out of Christianity. The Ten Commandments have provided a life guide for those who have followed the Christian religion for over two thousand years, and to be fair, there is an essential goodness therein.

They were clearly framed around those human beings who were presumed to be absolutely perfect, and that's where they came unstuck.

Because human beings aren't like that at all; we were never made that way!

I suppose the Ten Commandments gave us something to aim at, to aspire to, in order to live a blameless existence, but they were never a practical handbrake on our more extreme naughtiness.

The Eleventh Commandment in our part of the world—and in most other Western societies—means simply "thou shalt not get caught." In Australia, it's almost a rite of passage because of our larrikin nature; an expectation that we'll eventually get caught behaving badly.

Indeed it's a snapshot of modern life today, an irreverent but realistic view of how most of the Ten Commandments are broken by almost everyone, every day. Yet honoring the Eleventh and getting caught isn't the end of the world. In this case it was merely the beginning.

John Terry Moore

Chapter 1
IN THE BEGINNING

MY FATHER, an Irishman, styled himself as the unequivocal head of our household, and he didn't care if he broke the Ten Commandments because he was the boss. He ruled the roost, and no one dared defy him, not even God himself.

My first memory of anything was my father yelling at me. I was only a little bloke, about six years old. I had a younger sister, Mia, and our little brother, Timmy, was a newborn. I'd gone to Mum, who was feeding him. She finished and showed me how to burp him. I was so pleased I'd done something right. I really loved Timmy. He looked so cute as I cuddled him. He grinned at me, so I leaned in and kissed him before handing him back to Mum.

"Benjamin, you fuckin' little poofter." Dad's voice came from the doorway. "Boys are supposed to be men. Ya don't kiss other boys!" he screamed. He knocked me off the chair onto the floor, and I cried with the shock and the pain of it. It was the first time anyone had hit me. Mum screamed back at him, but the old man laughed at her. "I'll raise these kids to be men, not pansies. Real men don't kiss other men."

There were similar instances as I grew older. I somehow survived because of what the old man made me—an arsehole like him. His behavior drove Mum and me closer, and while I resisted his upbringing, I suppose a certain amount of conditioning took place over which I had no control.

Chapter 2
COLLEGE—AN EDUCATION IN LIFE

I LIKED gay people. Many of them had a struggle with their families, like I had, but for different reasons. The gay kids I met in college had mostly been damaged in one way or another in the process of coming out, and I was a straight boy brought up in a household with a violent father. I think I originally became friends with gay guys deliberately to antagonize Dad. He was a beer-swilling, foul-mouthed fuckhead who hated "poofters" as a matter of principle. "When you have a name like O'Connor, you have to fight for yer rights," he said. "A man can't even have a peaceful drink without some do-gooder or poof havin' something to say about it. And what's more, these Chinks, Indians, and all these Muslims need blowin' away. They'd steal the food off yer table, even take the beer outta ya fridge, and that's serious."

My gay mate Kenny Ho wanted to meet Dad "to see if people like him really exist" or whether

I was exaggerating. His eyes nearly fell out of his head when I introduced him one Friday night. Dad and his fucktard mates were in the garage, half of which had been converted into his playroom. There were green streamers hanging everywhere from the roof; St. Patrick's Day was a few days away, and they were working up to it.

"You wanna drink, sissy boy?" Dad asked Kenny.

"Oh, I'll have a soft drink, thank you, Mr. O'Connor."

"A soft drink."

"I'll have the same, Dad," I said, trying to make Kenny feel better.

"Listen, real men drink beer or whisky. There's none of that other shit here. By the way, where do you come from?" The room fell silent for once, and I thought here it comes, the full-on racial taunts were about to start. I thought perhaps we shouldn't hang around much longer when Kenny took over.

"I'm Australian, Mr. O'Connor," he said with a note of pride. "Fourth generation actually. My family originally came from China. We're immigrants, like your family, Mr. O'Connor, but I think our mob's been here a little longer than yours. Thanks for your hospitality. Enjoy St. Patrick's Day."

I couldn't contain myself; I giggled uncontrollably as we walked outside. Dad had been cut off at the pass so decisively he was lost for words. I grabbed a change of clothes before he went completely crazy. Mum had agreed I could have a weekend with Kenny and his family. Anything sounded better than Dad on the warpath.

As it turned out, that was the beginning of my real education. We greeted Kenny's parents, then walked past them to the stairs. Kenny reigned supreme on the top floor. He was an only child and had his every whim catered for. Mumsie and Daddypoos left him alone, never questioned him at all unless his academic performance faltered. He was a brilliant kid, and he was smart enough to study when he had to.

I'd been sexually active with several girls, but when Kenny got me home and offered to blow me, I accepted. This time it wasn't to upset Dad. This time it was for me. I was sick to death of chicks who wanted to "go steady" and others who were deliberately trying to trap guys so they could be trophy wives with a four bedroom brick veneer and a German car in the driveway. He really knew what he was doing, wrapping his lips around my dick and taking me to heaven. I glanced casually at him as he really got into it but freaked when he dropped his own trousers.

"I'm not gay, Kenny. You know that, don't you?" I said.

"Who cares?" Kenny grinned. He was a really good-looking bloke, quite well-built and rather stockier than most Asian guys. "Listen, we're having fun. My guess is you're not even bi. The chicks are all over you like a rash, and you do have a reputation for sticking your dick in everyone who says yes."

I laughed at him. He was a crazy guy, and we were great mates, but I'd allowed my sex drive and my curiosity to get the better of me. Not that I was complaining. It was true that guys gave better head than chicks. At least Kenny did.

But it did worry me a little—because underneath it all, I really enjoyed this shit.

Chapter 3
MUM

As IT turns out, Mum has been the only woman I've ever loved.

Dad's alcoholism got worse, and a few weeks after my hookup with Kenny, it all came to a head. His mongrel mates left for the night, and he stormed in the back door, yelling for his dinner, forgetting Mum was working night shift at the hospital after leaving a plate for him to microwave. He screamed for Mia to look after him. "Women were put on this earth to make sure the menfolk don't have to cook their own fucking meal," he roared and punched open her door to find the room empty. Next was Timmy's door, with the same result. He thought he'd be cunning in my case, opening my door quietly, but it didn't work because I was already outside shepherding my sister and brother over the fence to Mrs. Donaldson next door. Lorna Donaldson was a gem, she did housework for Mum, cash in hand, and was the only human being to whom Dad showed any fear. She made us cups of Milo and fed us with fruitcake, which calmed us down, helping us forget the tirade of ugliness from our father, who we could still hear yelling at no one next door.

The lights from Mum's car reflected in Mrs. Donaldson's kitchen window as she swung into our driveway, and I sprang out of my chair and hit the ground running. I had a feeling something bad was about to happen; Dad was the worst I'd ever seen him, and Mum was about to walk into a shitstorm.

I made it to the kitchen door as my father swung a punch at Mum's head. I flew in between them and hit him in the stomach as hard as I could, winding him, his fist connecting with Mum but most of the power gone. A flash lit up the room as Mrs. Donaldson recorded the moment on her iPhone, with my siblings looking on, terrified. Mum sank to her knees, sobbing both with pain and the realization that her marriage was over. Dad stumbled to his feet and charged toward me as the flashing blue lights of the cops filled the house and feet ran along the veranda, while Lorna Donaldson bravely recorded every moment.

The cops had Dad in handcuffs before he could do any more damage, but the noise level didn't drop—it increased. The look on Mum's face said it all; Dad was intent on waking the street so all the gossipy neighbors could witness her shame, trying to hurt her as much as possible, physically and mentally. The three of us kids ran over and hugged her, desperately trying to stop her pain— probably not succeeding, but at least she knew we loved her.

She straightened up, pointing to the kitchen table, and we sat down, Mrs. Donaldson joining us. "Thank you so much, Lorna," Mum said, "for keeping them safe. If you hadn't been here, goodness knows what may have happened."

"We're a good team, missus."

Chapter 4
STRUGGLE

MUM GOT me to the end of that college year, but it was obvious I couldn't go to university even if I wanted to. Mia and Timmy needed to get their VCE, so it was my turn now to take on the world and help Mum. She had help from Centrelink, and her nursing salary paid the mortgage, but we had to eat, and her savings were running out. She'd bought Dad's share of the house, and with the help of a friendly bank manager, which is a rarity, she refinanced it. Dad eventually declared himself bankrupt in his business as a builder, and Mum saw almost nothing toward the upkeep of Mia and Timmy. She worked long hours for modest wages, Mia worked in a day care center as a helper, while Timmy was the best little housekeeper ever! He could (and still does) create nice meals out of nothing. I shadowed the big supermarkets, even began working in one near home so I could have access to the free chuck-outs of food, which found their way straight to our table in many cases. The old expression "hand to mouth" was never more appropriate than in our case.

I cursed my old man for his lack of interest and total absence of financial support, but Mum and I agreed our independence was worth much more than the potential of more violence in the kids' lives. I was a tough prick. Nothing the old man could say or do scared me in the slightest, and I managed to tell him so every time I ran into him. Constant conditioning had forced me to live up to his adage. "The world is full of cunts," he'd said. "The only way to survive is to be a bigger cunt than they are."

It hadn't worked for my father, but I knew I had to be tough as I struggled to make a living for our family. I was quite handy with mechanical things, and I was given a really good heavy-duty rotary mower by an aged neighbor with no further use for it, as he was moving to assisted living. O'Connor Home Maintenance kept me busy during daylight hours, and I worked at Woolworths on the evening shift, stocking shelves.

I was sweating my guts out one day on a vacant block of land behind my new mower when this smartly dressed dude waved me over.

"Yeah," I said, "what do you want?"

"Why don't you turn that fucking thing off so we can talk," he yelled.

He looked familiar, and I thought he might be from a local real estate agency. He was youngish, maybe in his early thirties, and seemed intent on holding up progress—my progress.

"You from the real estate people?" I asked.

"I'm the owner, Andrew Smithson."

I remembered him now. He was one of the upwardly mobile young Turks around town, his perfect features everywhere on the internet and the newspaper, probably making squillions out of real-estate sales in a boom that seemed to go on forever. I read everything I could lay my hands on when I had time. I knew somehow my family would beat the poverty cycle and I could move on to something a bit easier. So I tried to keep up with what was going on around me in lieu of a university education.

"I've been watching you," he said, a smile on his perfect face.

"You want my body or something?" I snarled at him.

He roared with laughter. "You'd need to clean yourself up first." He smirked. "No, I came to offer you a job."

"What as," I said as forcefully as I could, "fucking office boy so you can hand me around?"

"Oooh, you do have a chip on your shoulder, and you're desperate, aren't you, working nights at Woolies to feed your mum and siblings and to educate them? But there is an easier way."

I knew he was deliberately winding me up, so I went all sugary sweet on him and pretended I was interested. He quoted a figure as a base salary that was more than I earned in a month, plus a percentage of each sale that would make your head spin.

"Why me?" I said, amazed.

"Several reasons. Like I said, you're desperate. You're also a hard worker, and you're an arsehole like me. You'll do well. I've got two people on staff at the moment who're fucking lazy, and I've put pressure on them. I know they'll both go on to other agencies eventually. By the time they're gone, you should be producing, so the opportunity's there. You got any decent clothes?"

"Only a funeral suit."

To my astonishment he peeled a thousand dollars off a wad of notes and handed it to me. "Go and get a decent suit and shirts, properly fitted, shoes and everything, a modern haircut, and your nails done. Give all your personal details to Gloria at this number. I expect you at work next Monday."

Chapter 5
SMITHSON REAL ESTATE

I REFUSED to allow the family to wind me up; they were ecstatic for me and seemed to think we'd go from rags to riches overnight. I knew there are really no freebies in life and working for this prick meant I shouldn't get ahead of myself. But I did allow Mum to fuss over me. She'd earned the right to dream a little, to come home and begin to enjoy her life again. She was leaving no stone unturned and decided I needed a consultant to look me over—Kenny.

"Gay men know how to dress," Mum said, "and they have a sense of style. Kenny is so beautiful. I'll bet some of it will rub off on you."

We hadn't seen much of each other lately, but he was still one of my best mates and could be relied on. He brought another guy with him, complete with enough hairdressing stuff to open a new salon at our place. They commandeered the dining room, and the results were spectacular. I could hardly recognize my own ugly self in the mirror.

"Okay," Kenny said, "thank you, Julian, we'll be in touch." He instructed me to pay Julian, who stood there, a silly look on his face, as I handed him his money. "Ben needs to shower now, and I'll finish the styling, thank you."

When I came out of the shower, Kenny dropped to his knees and blew me as if it was all part of the normal service. Thank Christ it was Saturday and everyone was out. I actually felt relaxed for the first time since this madness had begun. Kenny styled and gelled my hair and showed me how to look after it.

"What about your license?" he asked.

"What about it? I still have one."

"Not your driver's license, your real-estate license. You'll need that to operate."

"Fuck, I didn't know about that."

"Look, I think they accelerate the process with new people, but I downloaded the forms necessary. Let's fill them out together."

My new boss was blown away. To have a newbie front up on the first day with his license application filled out was unheard-of. "Unfortunately, you have to do some study before you'll need this," he said seriously, "but we'll fast-track you as much as possible. In the meantime, I want you to be my shadow. Watch me, and if you don't understand anything, ask, right?"

I nodded, aware I had much to learn.

Gloria was Andrew's PA, a bosomy forty-something chick who looked me over like I was this week's sacrificial lamb. I wondered if I'd have to throw her the odd fuck to get anywhere

in the future, but in the meantime, I homed in on
her as the best source of information on how the
place ran, who was up who, and how the industry
worked.

To my utter surprise, Gloria was a very nice
person, which certainly didn't fit in with my new
boss's lack of character. Nor did it fit the real-estate image as a whole, at least my perception of
it. She was enthusiastic to a fault and explained
the paper trail and legal requirements in the first
few days. I discovered that she held a license
herself and could fill in for any of the salespeople in a flash. It took me a few days, but I finally
worked out what motivated her—money, pure and
simple. Yes, she probably loved a bit of cock, but
that was quite secondary to earning a dollar. She
drove her "baby," an aged Mercedes sedan with a
big V8 engine and totally inappropriate in today's
energy-focused world. But she liked nice things,
and besides, every time she turned the key I think
she got her jollies. I made a mental note not to get
anywhere near the driver's seat; it was probably
permanently damp.

My boss, Andrew, reckoned I was a quick
learner. "Listings drive the business. If we don't
have anything to sell, we might as well close up
shop. It's a matter of getting to the seller first.
Drop everything and get there fast." He looked
at me with a crooked grin on his film-star face a
few weeks into my "cadetship." "Run this scenario through your mind," he said. "You have your
homework done on the way, as we discussed, you
know the prices other properties are bringing in

the immediate area, and Mr. and Mrs. Fuckwit want a ludicrous amount no cunt in their right mind would pay for what's probably a heap of shit, needs paint, repairs, and throwing half their junk out to make it look bigger. So, what would you do?"

"Agree with them," I said. "Sign them up at their price and get sole agency for at least sixty days. Then when it doesn't sell, blame the market and get their asking price back where it should've been in the first place. From day one, work out what turns them on. If the little woman takes a fancy, string her along, make her your best friend. Tell her she looks twenty years younger than she really is and she'll eat out of your hand. Or maybe it's hubby who fancies a bit of rogering on the side. Tell him he's hot, admire his fucking vegetable garden or whatever else turns him on, but use him to retain this business."

Andrew looked at me in sheer admiration, a smile on his handsome face. "But I want you to think about this: you have the potential to ruin my business, ruin me and yourself to the point we could never work in this town again, if you don't honor the Eleventh Commandment."

"What the fuck's that?"

"Think of the Ten Commandments, then add one more—Thou Shalt Not Get Caught."

Chapter 6
WHEELING AND DEALING

I MADE salesman with my license in record time and was thrust into the melee of selling residential real estate. For the first few months I leveled with clients, claiming inexperience, and referred everything back to Andrew, who beamed in appreciation.

"You're going well," he said. "But remember to cover your tracks. You seem to have a sixth sense. Use it. None of the riches will be worth anything if we end up in court."

I thought about what he'd said as I signed the lease papers for my new vehicle—a BMW X5 SUV. Customers expected me to arrive in style. After all, my sensible little Toyota Corolla would telegraph the opposite of success, so I signed up for this bloody great diesel barge.

Andrew's strategy was to grow Smithson Real Estate as the first stop in our town for upmarket listings. "These places take longer to sell, Benny boy, but they have a halo effect on the remainder of our business, and one of those a month is really all we need to be into profit. The top end of town are up themselves. Nothing new about that except, in the majority of cases, it's all show and no go. They have these huge monstrosities of homes, European cars, the best clothes—usually everything they wear, drive, or live in is owned by the banks or finance companies."

"Well, we do have Chinese investors looking for exactly that type of real estate," I said.

"Bingo," he said. "Now you know why Gloria speaks both Cantonese and Mandarin."

I thought about my Chinese contacts, who had eagerly attached themselves to me because I probably had more listings from the top end of town than anyone else, as I drove up the hill to see Margaret Dennison. I rang the doorbell, and a bloke in a collar and tie answered.

"I have an appointment with Mrs. Dennison," I said, and he grinned, pointing toward the front of the house. "Good luck, mate. She's in the Big Room."

Margaret Dennison was easy to read. She was a snob through and through. Her late husband, Bill Dennison, came from one of the district's old-money families. But Bill was a gambler. He loved the poker machines, the horses, the dogs, and managed to fritter away millions while Margaret had her lady friends around for tea. She wanted to sell the huge old mansion "Because it's too large for me now Bill has gone," she said, sniffling into a lace hanky.

That was top of town speak for "I've run out of money," I realized, so she'd be looking for a good earn to fund the remainder of her retirement. "I need to assess the property thoroughly," I said, "so we can establish a sale price. Could you show me around?"

"Eric will help you. Shall we reconvene here in thirty minutes? I have an appointment at twelve."

Eric confirmed she was desperate—she'd run up accounts everywhere, and he hadn't been paid for weeks. In fact he was returning to his old job of driving limousines for a living, so Margaret would have to make her own meals. "Even do the vacuuming," he said and laughed.

"Would she know how to turn it on?" I asked in disbelief.

"Probably not, but she'll con someone to do it for her. She's an expert."

The place was probably fifty years old, needing kitchen and bathroom renovations and a garden makeover. Its greatest feature was the magnificent views up and down the coast, and the address itself was popular with executives.

"I think around three million, Ben. What do you think?" Margaret Dennison said, sitting back in her winged armchair, probably a Dennison family heirloom.

"Margaret, anything is possible, but the house and garden need work. It would be a long-term project at that price, which would be attainable after spending, I'd suggest, around two hundred thousand. I'd say a three-year project. Yes, that would do it."

She looked at me with disdain, and I wondered if I'd lost the business. "No, I need to move on

quickly now I'm a widow," she said. "I need something smaller, in a nice area of course. What do you
think we could achieve for an 'as is' sale?"

Bingo, I thought and smiled sweetly at her. "I
think we should ask one point nine million, and
we should have a reasonably prompt result."

I signed her up on the spot and got the details
of her solicitor for the Section 32. When I saw the
document a few days later, I was shocked. The
Dennison family had a gigantic reverse mortgage
from the bank, which didn't give old Margaret
much wriggle room at all. Maybe enough to buy a
reasonable unit in a nice suburb, but certainly not
enough to fund her lifestyle.

I put out the feelers to one of our Chinese contacts, and he was interested—bloody interested—
and after an inspection put in a sensible offer. I
rang Margaret and asked if I could call around on
my way home. "I have some news which you may
be pleased to review."

"A sensible offer, I hope, Benjamin."

"I think so. See you shortly."

I drove in, and this time she opened the door
herself and ushered me into the nice little sitting
room off the kitchen area. "We've had an offer
of one million, eight hundred and fifty thousand,
Margaret," I said, "but it is the only offer after
some forty people have inspected the property."

"Oh, I suppose one has to be sensible about
these things. After all it's not a market that *ordinary* people could afford. May I ask who the buyer
is? Lovely if it was one of the old families."

"Actually it's Mr. Lee, a Shanghai broker. We know him quite well."

I thought the old girl was going to leap out of the chair. "Oh, how *vulgar*. No, no, never. I could never agree to that," she shouted, almost spitting the words out. "What would people think, our lovely family home going to those terrible creatures? Our standards are dropping everywhere. No, I'm sorry, Benjamin, that is completely unacceptable. Let yourself out. I need to gather my wits."

I sat there with my mouth open; then realizing I'd been dismissed, I said something like "We'll be in touch" as I walked swiftly outside. I couldn't believe the stupid old bitch. The market had slowed for mansions, and I was certain there wasn't anything else in the offing.

When I walked into the office in the morning, Andrew was happier than I thought he deserved to be. We went over the strategy, and nothing was out of place. The silly old cunt had let her snobbery and racism get the better of her.

"What the fuck do we do now?" I asked my boss, who seemed as cool as a cucumber.

"We use up the advertising budget she agreed to and report back each week," he said. "She'll come back to the field. With that level of debt around her, she won't last long. You have any other heads on the place?"

"No, of course not. That market's flat. No one but the Chinese are interested. About the only other interested parties would be more Chinese."

I admit I almost forgot about the Dennison property after that. I faithfully contacted her each week, the level of exasperation more and more evident each time we spoke. Finally one Monday morning she snapped, and I was ready for her.

"You'd best accept that offer," she said, "I simply don't have time to dilly-daddle. The racing season is nearly upon us. I hate to do this, but time is of the essence."

Yes, you have creditors breathing down your ugly old neck.

"Very well, Margaret, I'll ring Mr. Lee and establish if the offer is still current." Her phone was an old landline, and she slammed the receiver down in my ear as I smiled at Andrew. He gave me the thumbs-up. I allowed an hour or so and rang her back.

"Yes," she snapped.

"Margaret, there's both good and bad news. Due to your hesitation, Mr. Lee had to look elsewhere for his clients, so he would be purchasing your property for stock, as it were. So his offer is now one point eight million even, which incidentally we think is still quite a good price." The language emanating from Margaret Dennison's mouth was, as Andrew said afterward, "Straight from the gutter, with no filter."

Settlement was in sixty days, and Andrew and I did the paperwork ourselves, a task Gloria would normally handle, but she was conveniently visiting her sister. Mr. Lee called in with two parcels, one for me, one for Andrew. I drove straight home and unwrapped the parcel in my bedroom. Five thousand dollars doesn't look all that much when it's in hundreds, but it was all there. I planned carefully what to do with it.

I hadn't done anything illegal, only something totally unethical.

That'll teach the old cunt to be racist, I thought, trying to justify my actions.

Chapter 7
TAMMY

I'D BEEN working bloody seven days a week since I became a fully-fledged salesman at Smithson's, having no time for me at all. I'd dated several women, all interested in the BMW but not very much in me. Getting laid was almost an impossibility, so I rang Kenny for some light relief. He was also a busy man; he had an online business run from his parents' garage, which he'd turned into an office and dispatch area. After one particular assignation, he told me we were taking a tour of the cottages.

"What bloody cottages? I need a head job, not more fucking real estate."

He pointed to his vehicle, a nondescript-looking Subaru. I got in, and we headed toward the river and parked discreetly away from a toilet block.

"Watch, Ben," he said. "When I'm busy and you're horny and the women aren't interested in your lovely cock, this is the alternative."

I began to think he was a little unhinged, but sure enough, I noticed a shadow slipping in through the "cottage" door. And another. A few minutes later they all left, but not before I recognized a guy from another agency.

"Jesus," I said, "I didn't know Grant Hopkins was gay."

"I think he's in a similar situation to you," Kenny said.

"Like me, straight?"

"No, I actually think he's gay, like a lot of the married guys on Grindr, but you both work in real estate and the hours are terrible. So if you're discreet and careful, you can call in on your way home from work."

MUM HAD been telling me for a while that the time was approaching when I should consider my own lifestyle rather than pouring money into the family home. But I was happy there, in a manner of speaking. Mum and I were like two old girl-friends. I told her everything about myself.

"I know you like Kenny. Is it serious?" Mum said with a smirk on her face.

"Mum, for the umpteenth time, I'm not gay," I said. "But you don't believe me!"

"Whatever floats your boat, dear. Nothing you could say or do would ever upset me. You're perfect in my eyes. The kids are growing up feeling good about themselves, and a mortgage-free existence is within reach, thanks to you."

Mum was right, though; it was time I spread my wings and got a place of my own. Mia was working as a hairdresser, and Timmy was in year twelve at school. Then, in the space of a week, my life took a decisive U-turn almost without me being involved.

I'd met Tammy Swift through Gloria. Tammy was her niece from the bush, and she'd recently come to live with her. Tammy had a similar start in life to me—her parents' marriage had also imploded. I'd listened to Gloria counseling her sister on the phone, so none of that stuff was a surprise. We'd been out a few times, and we seemed compatible enough, including in the bedroom. She wasn't a Rhodes Scholar, but she wasn't dumb either. We appeared to like each other. I actually enjoyed having someone around who seemed unpretentious for a change, who liked to cook and was interested more in the basics than some of the other fucking airheads I'd dated who spent more time worrying about their posts on social media than even breathing.

Tammy was really pretty without being beautiful, with close-cropped dark brown hair and quite a happy nature. Dating her casually was great, and it might have stayed that way—until a particular night when we'd gone out to the pictures.

"What's wrong?" I asked as we climbed into the Beemer after the movie. "You look a bit sad."

"Nothing's wrong," Tammy said.

"You're pregnant, aren't you?"

"Yes," she said, with an astonished look. "How did you know?"

"Oh, my boss calls it a sixth sense."

She put her head down, started weeping, and then won serious Brownie points by telling the truth.

"I fell pregnant before I left home, so obviously you're not the father, Ben. I'm very sorry for wasting your time. I've decided to keep the baby, so if you'll drive me home, I'll get on with my life."

"Who's going to look after you?"

"Auntie Gloria will help. She was upset I hadn't told you already. I didn't because we seemed to be having a good time, but all good things come to an end. So once again I'm sorry, but it's over."

"I'll look after you and the child," I said. "Every kid deserves a family around them. Mum and I raised Mia and Timmy when the old man pissed off, and frankly I wouldn't mind doing it again. It's time I had my own family and my own place."

"I couldn't ask you to do that. It's not fair on you."

"Do you know who the father is?"

She blushed. "No, I don't," she whispered, embarrassed. "There's too many to ask to take a test, and it wouldn't look good for Mum. Dad wouldn't care. He called me a slut anyway and tried to rape me one night when he was drunk. That's why they split up. It's best to leave it alone."

"Tammy, I'll look after you, and between us we'll give the child a home. I certainly know what it's like not to be wanted."

Gloria was grateful but careful when we told her. "Are you sure about this, Benny?" she said. "It's a big responsibility and a real change in your lifestyle."

"I know, but I want to do this, Gloria. It's important to me."

"Well, okay, but there's one thing I want you to do before you go one step further."

"What's that?"

"I'll get my legal bloke to draw up a pre-nuptial agreement. If things don't work out, then you're protected. That's the least my family can do for you."

Chapter 8
CASA O'CONNOR

MY PHONE snarled at me, and a heavily accented voice asked for "Mr. O'Connor, *danke*."

"Speaking."

I was aware I was speaking to a German woman struggling with her English, and I apologized because I was an Australian bloke struggling with German. She'd found my name on the internet and asked could I call around to an address in New Hampton, our town's most affluent suburb. Ten minutes later I was at the front door, which was opened by a woman I reckoned was in her early seventies, smartly dressed and comfortable looking.

"Come in," she said, pointing to the kitchen area. "My name is Helga." Her English was more understandable than on the phone. "My brother Hans, he pass away two weeks ago. The funeral was yesterday. My family is from Stuttgart. I have no one. My husband pass away last year, both my children very busy in their careers, so I am here to wind up his affairs."

"I'm very sorry for your loss," I said, meaning it for once. "What can I do to help?"

"Must sell the house quickly so I can finish here," she said. "I need to finalize in two weeks. My daughter will marry for the second time. She has good man this time, and I must be there to help."

I thought quickly. I couldn't misrepresent the true sale price—I'd go to jail if I did that. Andrew, my boss, would smell the money if I told him, so I decided I'd try being honest.

"Helga, can I inspect?" I asked, waving my hand above me to signify the remainder of the house.

"Of course."

The further I went, the more impressed I became. The condition of the place was stunning. It was perfectly maintained.

"Hans was an engineer," she said. "He never marry. Very careful with everything."

The house sat on a large block, in itself valuable for its potential to be subdivided later on. It had six bedrooms and three bathrooms, like a small hotel, garaging for four vehicles, and the very latest in kitchen appliances.

Our Helga wasn't fucking about. "I sell to you for seven hundred thousand Australian dollars," she said. "Can you transfer money in two weeks?"

I nearly wet myself with excitement. The bloody place was worth three times that amount, and she knew it. She'd plucked a number out of the air, and I nodded. I had work to do. I knew I couldn't lay my hands on that sort of dough without help, so I rang Gloria.

"I need some help, please. Can you meet me for coffee?"

We sat outside in the al fresco area of a little restaurant, and I explained my problem to her. Her face creased with pleasure at the thought that we had the potential to drill it up Andrew Smithson—"As long as we are really, really careful. Don't tell a soul until it's over," she whispered, "he has ears everywhere." Then, almost in the same sentence, "Ben, do you love Tammy?"

I looked at her with my mouth open, really quite stupidly. She smiled, dropped her shoulders, and then grinned. "I should have more sense, asking that question of a real-estate agent, shouldn't I?" she said. "But you've looked after Tammy so well you deserve to have a place of your own. Remember, if cuntface Andrew asks how you came to buy the house, tell him the truth. He'll be livid he missed out, and he'll try to fire you. If he does, tell him you and I will go out on our own and take his business with us. That would be so much fun."

I'd been saving well but had nowhere near enough for a deposit. Not only did Gloria make up the balance with a simple promissory note between us, she took me to a finance broker friend who owed Gloria big-time for the business she'd sent his way over the years.

"I wondered when you'd catch up with me, Gloria," he said and quoted an interest figure.

Gloria erupted and began shouting. "You evil bastard," she roared. "I said no income for you on this one, and I bloody meant it! How could you try this shit on me? You of all people, who have probably banked millions from the deals I've sent you."

"But I have to cover costs, Gloria."

"You have no fucking costs on this one, you greedy prick. Dip into your jam jar, or you'll never get another dollar of my business."

The guy made some more calculations, and Gloria smiled for the first time. "That's more like it, Geoffrey," she purred. "Prepare the documents. You have a week. And Geoffrey?"

"Yes, Gloria?"

"This is confidential. Smithson mustn't know about this, right?"

"Understood, Gloria. I'd better get on with it."

Gloria turned to me with a wicked smile on her face. "What do sperm and real-estate agents have in common?" she asked quietly.

I shook my head "dunno." There was a punch line there somewhere, but my focus had been elsewhere in this exercise.

"Both have a million-to-one chance of becoming a human being."

WE MOVED in. The furniture stayed in place because Helga included it in the sale. While it was heavy and dark looking, I thought it suited the European feel of the house. Tammy didn't like it, wondering why we didn't have lovely IKEA stuff to lighten up the rooms.

"Because we can't afford it," I said, so she had a fit of the sulks. It wasn't until I was talking to Gloria a couple of days later that I realized she'd given her the same message.

"Don't worry, Benny boy. Pregnant sheilas can be real bitches. She'll get over it."

Mum, Mia, and Timmy were over the moon, however. They loved everything about the house and said so. Each of them had their bedroom marked out, even though they had the old family home to live in. Their remarks didn't suit Tammy either, but that was okay. Once again she'd get over it; she always did.

"We miss you, love," Mum said, "but you have to live your own life now. Are you happy, Ben?"

"Yeah, why?" I asked.

"Possessions don't mean much unless there's love under the roof. There was precious little of that with Dad. How we didn't come unstuck earlier is a miracle."

I looked at my mother in wonder. All this hearts-and-flowers shit got in the way of what else was going on in the world. I certainly didn't have time for any of it.

It was some months before Andrew Smithson found out what I'd done. I was summoned into his office, where he proceeded to ream me out for my unethical dealing and nondisclosure of the property in which I was now resident.

"I should dispense with your services," he screamed, the veins standing out in his still-perfect face, which I'd realized lately had become a botox playground.

"Why don't you let me go, Andrew," I said, full of confidence. "I'd probably start up again with Gloria. We'd have a right old time with your customer database."

His volume increased threefold. I was sure at this stage Andrew would have a heart attack or stroke and solve everyone's problems.

"You trained me so well, Andy Pandy," I said, knowing he hated the nickname Gloria had created for him. "If you sack me, I also take with me the knowledge and some evidence of *your* dealings over the years, and we wouldn't like that, would we?"

He wasn't listening. "How much did you pay for that place?"

"Seven hundred."

"Jesus, it's worth at least three times that. Where's my cut?"

"Fuck off. I have to live somewhere. I could ask you for some lolly for the place you happen to be living in."

"You weren't even working here when I bought it."

"You're a greedy prick, Andy, and so am I, so let's get on with it."

Chapter 9
PETER

TAMMY WAS doing it hard; her legs had swollen, and she was now overdue by her own calculations. It was around midnight when her water broke, and we were on our way to the hospital. She was in labor for the next few hours. When I called in at 9:00 a.m., I was gowned up and allowed to watch as she delivered a little boy. He was wrinkled like a little old man covered in goo but responded to a tap on the back and started roaring his head off. I looked at him in wonder. I wasn't the birth father, but he was my son, of that I was sure.

Even Tammy seemed softer, gentler, as we discussed what to call him. "I like Peter," she said. My eyes nearly fell out of my head. Her choice was actually my choice; it couldn't be better.

"Peter O'Connor," Tammy said. "It has a nice sound to it."

"You can't give him my name. I'm not his father."

Tammy was adamant. "If it hadn't been for you, Ben, he'd have no future, no home, nothing.

It was meant to be—the birth certificate will show 'father unknown,' but his surname will be O'Connor. I know that's how it should be."

I looked at Tammy in a new light. Motherhood became her. She was nice to be around, and we seemed to be heading in the right direction. I know Mum was still a bit bemused at my relationship with Tammy—but to be honest, it suited both of us. I couldn't stand the thought of all that gooey love stuff, the fucking candlelit dinners, the romantic shit on birthdays, Valentine's Day, and any other fucking excuse of a day for losing your fucking mind to all that stupid shit. My parents did that once, according to Mum, and look where it got them.

But the crowning piece of bullshit is getting married, for Christ's sake. Standing up in fucking hired clobber while the little missus is there in a once-only dress that cost enough to feed a small nation for a year. And the celebrant telling lies on their behalf: how they love each other and how perfect their lovely life is when you know both of them will be out getting their rocks off with someone else as soon as the honeymoon is over. The Eleventh Commandment all over again.

In the meantime, our son was growing like a weed. I could almost see him getting bigger. From a very early age, he slept all night. I was the early riser, so it was no effort to change and feed him. I knew he was going to be smart; he watched everything I did and tried to copy me, which for a baby is pretty remarkable.

Tammy began to change around his third birthday. She was still a really good, attentive mother. Peter was clean, well fed, and looked after, but Tammy seemed bored.

"Would you like another one," I said, pointing to Peter, who was evidence of our team effort.

She blew me off like a cyclone. "No," she snapped. "One is enough, thank you. I have a life of slavery already. I don't want to be tied down for the rest of my life."

I stopped myself from saying something I'd regret, but I took notice of the warning. Tammy likened herself to a brood mare rather than quite the clever young woman she was. I tried to interest her in clubs or mother's groups, but she thought I was winding her up rather than helping her.

"Listen, Ben," she said. "I can think for myself, and there's a lot of stuff out there I can do if I put my mind to it. We may have to make arrangements for childcare quite soon."

Gloria loved Peter, and the feeling was mutual. At three years old he squealed with delight when Gloria appeared. She reckoned he was a gifted kid, and we should get him tested because he might qualify for an extension of the normal learning program, being shadowed by a mentor to ensure he reached his full potential.

"Jesus, Gloria," I said, "he's only three years old. You'll have him attending university as a ten-year-old."

"Well, your mother agrees with me. Stick around sometime and listen, Ben." She grinned, thumping me in the guts and nearly winding me.

"The trouble with real-estate salesmen is they never listen to any bloody thing. You might learn something if you listened to your own son."

I was home early for once one evening. Tammy had gone out with a girlfriend, and Mum was babysitting. I opened the back door quietly because I could hear these voices that seemed deep in conversation. I wondered who was sitting in the kitchen with Mum, but there was just... Peter.

"Hello, Dad," he yelled, jumping down from the stool where he'd been perched and running over for a cuddle. He and I were closer than ever. True love, I thought, was showing kids they were wanted and loved, particularly by the father figure in the house.

"You had your tea yet?" I asked.

"Yes, Dad. Fish and chips and salad. Granny cooked it."

"Okay, why don't you get ready for bed. I'll turn the shower on."

Ten minutes later, he was tucked into bed. He wanted to know how many houses I'd sold and how much money I'd earned for the day!

Mum stood at the doorway, laughing. "I'm afraid he's well past *Blinky Bill* and other bedtime stories, dear." But even little child prodigies get tired, and a few minutes later he was sound asleep, his thumb in his mouth.

"How long has this been going on?" I said to Mum. "Gloria said I should tune in more, but he's a real brain, isn't he?"

"Yes." Mum smiled at me. "He's like an old man. He's years ahead in some things but still a little boy in others."

"He's only three, Mum."

"Think about it," Mum said. "Think of all the good he could do in the world if you give him the opportunity."

I agreed, but I was troubled, and I told Mum about Tammy's current mindset.

"It will probably pass, dear," she said. "But you've spoilt Tammy. She needs to earn some money and be independent instead of pouring the housekeeping funds down the mouths of poker machines."

"Mum," I said, "that's awful."

She straightened herself up and apologized. "I'm sorry, love. I shouldn't interfere, but I worry about you at times."

"Mum," I asked, "what would happen if either Tammy or me or both of us were in an accident? What would happen to Peter?"

"I'd have him in a heartbeat. So would Mia and Timmy. Perhaps you should put something in writing."

Chapter 10
ON THE WAY HOME

I FELT pretty good for a while today; I'd signed up a two-and-a-half-million-dollar house and land package, which would put food on the table and get Tammy off my back for another week or so, or until she emptied the grocery account playing poker machines. I tried reasoning with her over her gambling, but it only got worse, and what little sex life I had dried up completely.

I drove down to the eastern side of a park I knew of, where the toilets were still old-fashioned things with a trough and stalls, and parked well away from the lights where no bastard could see my car or the plates. A little SUV pulled in not far from the entrance, and the driver was out of the vehicle and inside the Gents before I could get a good look at him. The glimpse I caught only told me he was young because he moved quickly, not like some of the old regulars I tried to avoid.

I strode inside promptly, since hanging around outside was asking for trouble. There was no sign of him except for a closed door on one stall. I

went to the trough and managed a leak—I had to
be careful as he could have been genuinely taking
a crap. I waited a few minutes, walked over, and
nudged the door open with my hand. He was sitting back, legs spread wide, with a smirk on his
face, long curly black hair, and a big stiffy, waiting for me. Without a word, I slipped inside and
dropped my cock out, and he went to town on it,
obviously enjoying himself.

He was only nineteen or twenty, but he knew
exactly what he was doing. No mucking about
with kissing and shit but focused on getting me
off. I felt the familiar tingle and came quickly. He
cleaned me with his tongue, and I buttoned up. I
cracked the door slightly, but there was someone
at the trough who must have sneaked in during the
head job. I froze, placing my finger over my lips,
and pointed over my shoulder so he understood
to be quiet. With a shuffle of shoe leather, the guy
departed, but my friend wanted more, holding up
his phone as I stepped out of the stall.

"You wanna catch up again? Give me your
number?"

"No."

He didn't answer, only hung his head and
closed the door firmly, cutting off contact. I walked
out, looking around carefully, but the coast was
clear. The coppers seldom had decoys anymore,
but they did watch the beats and could do you for
loitering.

We had a family friend who got done with the
lot. Started something with a police decoy at the
trough. The copper booked him, a married guy

with three grown-up kids and a cunt of a missus who hated him. The poor guy had to appear at court, but he paid the reporter from the local newspaper a small fortune and the story didn't appear. Got him in the long run, though; he got cancer and died only nine months later. He was a good mate. Like me, he was a straight guy who had sex with other guys, and it caught up with him. I hoped I'd never get myself in that situation. Grindr was safer, but that's really for the gay guys, and I didn't like the idea of some nosy prick finding the app on my phone.

When I got home, Tammy was actually home but in one of her moods. Peter was in bed, and she wanted to be argumentative.

"Where've you been? You're late again," she said as I walked in.

"Oh, thank you for asking," I answered. "I had a lovely day, thank you. I signed up the Wang property tonight for two-and-a-half million, so we'll eat well again next month."

"I still don't see why you can't work proper hours," she said. "Craig Browning works over at Milson's, and Jasmine says he's always home around six o'clock."

"Craig Browning is a fucking loser, that's why he's home early," I snapped. "He's an idiot. He likes to fuck about and theorize and talk bullshit. It's so easy to take listings off him, it's like taking candy from a kid. So what do you want, Tammy, a good income like we have or me home every night at the right time?"

She ignored my version of the truth and pointed to a plate with a plastic cover. "Microwave," she said and went into the lounge room. I ate my meal, which I must admit was nice. She was still gabbing on her mobile, so I put my stuff in the dishwasher and went out to my shed in the backyard.

My hand caressed the little sliding panel where my stash was hidden; It was always soothing to smoke a joint, like a welcome nightcap that helped me sleep and put up with Tammy's spells of boredom. It was also a reward for surviving the years of yelling and screaming from my old man as he attacked me, my sister, my young brother, or Mum.

And it helped me deal with some other stuff I preferred not to think about—like knowing I was a straight guy who liked women but who also liked blow jobs from guys.

Chapter 11
THE WHEEL TURNS

ANDREW HAD forgiven me fairly quickly; I was generating too much lovely lolly for him to be concerned over a few dollars he hadn't been quick enough to lay his hands on before I did. Anyway, I was living in the place. It wasn't as if I'd sold it and made a profit.

The dough kept on rolling in. We made quite a bit of black money the tax office didn't know about, so I helped Mum pay her house off, and my sister and brother helped as well. The teamwork was amazing. I was really proud of Mia and Timmy. They were both still living at home, but they looked after Mum. Neither of them talked about finances. They contributed equally into a jar every week, and the old house ran along. I paid the promissory note out to Gloria and started working away on my own home loan.

Tammy seemed even more unsettled over time, though. I thought I understood what it was like not to belong somewhere—hence her addiction to poker machines—so I started taking her out a little more. We went to my favorite restaurant in the northern part of town, which has beautiful food and a very cosmopolitan atmosphere, and she seemed to enjoy herself.

"I do worry about you," I said. "You don't seem to have many friends these days, and you probably need a career or even some voluntary work to keep you ticking over."

"I'm all right," she said. "I'm quite keen to become a nursing aide, but I'll need to do some training."

"Mum could help you there."

"I'd like to do something for myself," she said in a very firm manner, her way of telling me not to interfere.

"Well, say the word," I said, ignoring her petulance. "If you need some more free time, Pete likes the day care place, and Mum, Mia, Timmy, or even Gloria can collect him if I'm busy."

Tammy looked thoughtful. "It's like an army, isn't it, with your family? He's a lucky kid."

She seemed to snap out of the doldrums a little, so I suggested a short holiday. This would be our first holiday as a family, and we flew to Cairns and on to Palm Cove for a week, taking Peter with us. I had a ball with him—walks along the beach with all the sights, smells, and sounds of the coast, which were all new, and the questions were endless. Tammy used the time to rest. She seemed to grow in confidence daily, which I thought was a good thing, although she still seemed a bit remote, like we were going in different directions. Midway through the week, I persuaded her to come down for breakfast with Peter and me, and she enjoyed it all: the buffet, the view out over the sea, and the interaction with staff and other guests.

We'd been without any real intimacy for a long while. I put it down to the normal ebb and flow that seemed to be part of all relationships from time to time. That night I tried my luck again, but she was asleep before the words were out of my mouth. I studied the ceiling, which was white with a crisscross pattern of plaster battens, and willed my dick to deflate once again. I wished I was at the park, or even better that Kenny had called around with those lovely fat lips of his to help me out. *Sometimes life's a real bastard.*

We arrived home midafternoon, and I disappeared to work to catch up with my recent sales. When I arrived home again, Tammy was out, but Mum was there. She fed Peter, and I readied him for bed.

"I liked our holiday, Dad," he said. "Can we go rock-hopping again? We could do it here and not even fly in a plane."

My son loved the simple things in life, like me. At times I did wonder if I was his genetic parent, but that wasn't possible. He'd worked out that the coastline near home was as full of similar marine wonderment as Palm Cove, and I promised I'd find a Sunday soon for an exploration.

Mum waved goodbye, and I thanked her and found myself some food.

Still no Tammy. Mum said she'd mentioned something about a job interview, but it was now 9:00 p.m., and I began to worry. Surely her future employer wouldn't keep her this late. I tried her mobile, but each time it went through to message bank.

I thought of the police. She'd never done anything like this before. It was completely out of character. No matter where she was, we always knew approximately when she'd be home. I went out to my shed and rolled a spliff for myself. It calmed me down, and I reasoned I would have heard by now if she'd been in an accident. I went to bed, where I tossed and turned, sleeping fitfully. Finally, at around 2:15 a.m., I heard her car in the drive, and I jumped out of bed.

"You all right?" I asked as she came in the door. "I was worried about you. I thought you might have phoned if you were going to be this late."

"Not now, Ben," she said. "We'll talk before you go to work. I'm sleeping in the other bedroom." My mouth hung open like a wet haversack. Tammy was laying down the law, which was good for her confidence, but she was treating me like a manservant instead of her partner. I knew something was up; she'd never slept anywhere else but in our bed unless she was ill, and she looked fine to me.

I rang Gloria early. "Look, I've got some issues at home I have to handle. Would you cover for me for a few hours?"

"Of course, Benny. I understand. See you later on."

Why do some people always know more about my affairs than I do? I thought to myself.

Tammy sat at the breakfast bar. I had no option but to listen; it was her show, not mine. "I've met someone, Ben," she said, "and I'm leaving."

I was shocked, but if I was realistic, the signs had been there for some time—the lack of intimacy in our relationship should have rung alarm bells earlier. A dreadful sadness swept over me. Tammy and I had come together because she was pregnant, and between us, we'd raised a wonderful little child. With all our shortcomings as a couple, we'd been successful raising a kid who was not only headed toward becoming a child prodigy, but who had a beautiful nature that even someone as fucked-up as me could appreciate. Suddenly the full implications of her decision hit me, and I readied myself for a fight, but she was ahead of me.

"I'm not taking Peter with me," she said in a measured, factual tone of voice. "I want him to stay here with you. I've realized I'm not very maternal at all. In fact I'm only going through the motions of motherhood. Peter will grow up to be an amazing person, but it will be thanks to you and your family. They love him, whereas I'm pretending, to be honest."

Tammy displayed no emotion, unlike me. I felt like my guts had been ripped out, and I cried. In one fell swoop, Tammy had destroyed our family. I would be a single man again, this time with a son—a son who wasn't mine by birth but who I adored anyway.

"You can't walk out on him like that," I said, my voice unsteady. "What happens when he sees you at the shops or wherever?"

"He won't," Tammy said. "We're moving interstate, to Western Australia, and we won't be returning here."

"So who is the new bloke?" I asked. "Do I know him?"

"My new partner is a lady," she said. "She's a nurse at Green Slopes Private, so even your mother doesn't know her. The deal is me by myself, no child, and I agreed. It was an easy decision for me. I told Aunt Gloria yesterday. I've been to her solicitor, and I've already signed away my rights as Peter's mother. I'm sorry, Ben, but as you say, that's the way the cookie crumbles. We've come all this way, nearly six years, but we never loved each other, did we? This time for me will be different, of that I'm sure. I'll have all my stuff out by late this afternoon."

Tammy calmly got to her feet and went upstairs, no doubt to begin packing. I ran to Peter's bedroom, and he was awake. I faced the nearly impossible task of telling my son his mother wouldn't be around anymore, and I steeled myself.

"Hey, little man, you sleep well?"

"Did Mum come home?"

"Yes, she did, but she's going again."

He looked at me like a wise little old man. *He knew before I did, and he's already worked out who really loves him.*

"Gran, Auntie Mia, and Uncle Timmy will help us, mate," I said.

"Can we go to Gran's place now, Dad?"

"What a good idea. We can have breakfast there."

Chapter 12
THE NEW OLD FAMILY

I SAT down with Mum while Peter plowed through a big breakfast, seemingly untroubled by the morning's sensational events. Timmy walked in as he was finishing up.

"Hey, Pete, you going to preschool today, or are you staying here to eat everything?"

"School, then I'll come home and eat your dinner."

"Come on, then, I've got a spare toothbrush and then we'll go."

I mouthed my thanks to Timmy. It was a testament to my family's interest in Peter that each of their three cars had a kid seat already fitted. He kissed me goodbye, then his grandmother, and ran out the door, apparently excited about the day ahead.

"What's the poor little bugger going to think?" I asked Mum. "We three kids know what it feels like to be abandoned, but at least we were teenagers when Dad left, and we were actually pleased to see him gone because of his violence. But Tammy has been a constant in his life, a good mother to boot, and suddenly she's walked out on him without any reason. Except in his mind it's probably his fault."

"Don't overdramatize it, love, and don't forget his level of intelligence. He's probably worked it out for himself already."

"But he's only a five-year-old. What do I tell him?"

"The truth when he asks the question, and he will. Your son simply needs to know he can rely on all of us to take up the slack, that we love him unconditionally, and we'll always be here for him. Don't lie to him to make him feel better. Even though he's a little man, he deserves to know the truth. Life will be much easier to handle if he knows where he stands from the outset."

It was beginning to sink in at last; my mind cleared a bit as I began to be practical once more. "Why don't you lease this place out," I said, "and move into my place. You'd get at least seven to eight hundred a week for it, and that could go straight into your superannuation. There's plenty of room, and being selfish, Peter would have his family around him all the time."

"What if you decide to take on another partner?" Mum said. "We'd be in the way."

"The likelihood of me getting involved with anyone else again is somewhere between nil and zero," I said, "so don't stress over that."

"Well, let's discuss it over dinner tonight," Mum said. "I don't think you'll have any opposition."

I ROARED out of Mum's driveway and drove home, hoping to catch Tammy before she left, but all I saw was her car disappearing at the end of the street. My first instinct was to follow, but my stubbornness and pride got in the way. I sighed to myself; I hadn't been strictly faithful, but I certainly never cheated on her with another woman, ever. I was hurt. It welled up inside me—my little family was broken, and it wouldn't ever be the same again. The feelings ran through my mind as I sat in the car, trying to motivate myself. Suddenly I was aware of another vehicle pulling in behind me, and I sighed. I needed whoever it was to move because I should really go into work.

I opened my door and looked into the eyes of my mate Kenny. No words were spoken, but he pulled me into an embrace, which made me feel as if the world wasn't such a cunt of a place after all.

"Your mum rang," he said, and I smiled at him. Mum reckoned Kenny always left me smiling, and I suppose she wasn't wrong in that respect. But even I wasn't expecting what happened next as Kenny shepherded me into my own bedroom and proceeded to undress me.

"Whaddya up to?" I protested. After all, a blow job didn't require removal of almost everything I was wearing. Kenny smiled, leaned in, and

kissed me. He smelled of an herbal essence or
something. Whatever it was, it was distinctively
Asian, and while I should've been stronger, I gave
in as Kenny swung over on top and rode me like a
bucking bronco. I didn't last long. After I finished,
he pulled the covers over us, and I slept—the best,
most peaceful sleep I'd had for a long, long time.

THE CHANGEOVER was seamless. I formally
adopted Peter, my place became our place, and
Peter had a family around him. Kenny was a fre-
quent visitor. Sometimes he even stayed the night,
siphoning me dry, which calmed me, rather than
pursuing anal, which I didn't care for all that much.
No one queried the strange relationship, not even
Mum, who smiled knowingly at me when I closed
the bedroom door. I was still straight. I knew that
and so did Kenny. We were fuck buddies and really close mates. Best mates in fact.

Chapter 13
HOW NOT TO BE A SUCCESS

Smithson Real Estate was flying. We'd had three consecutive record months, and the signs of success were everywhere. Two new sales staff were hired, and I was made sales manager. Gloria and I bought into the business, having stood over "Andy Pandy" threatening to start our own agency. He caved because he knew we'd be successful; Gloria and I were a great team, and the risk to his business was obvious.

Andrew backed off much of the day-to-day matters. He bought himself a Jaguar, and for all intents and purposes, he was content to let Gloria and me run the business. He did, however, decide we needed to treat ourselves at least once a week. "Why not have a good time while the good times last?" he said.

When I asked Gloria if she wanted to party on, she laughed at me. I didn't think it was particularly funny, but she decided I'd better be prepared for what lay ahead.

"Ben, dear," she said with a smile, "it's red-neck paradise, all men, some in business like Andy, some well-to-do tradies, almost all of them self-employed, determined to let off some steam because they can. Be careful, please, because they get pretty wild at the Business Club."

"We park our vehicles—no driving any-where," Andrew instructed as Gloria took posses-sion of our keys and called a cab a bit before mid-day on Friday. "Playtime, Benny boy." He smiled as he directed the driver to an industrial area only ten minutes from the office.

I looked in disbelief as we pulled up in the driveway of a motor repair business: busy, typi-cally noisy, with air compressors, revving engines, and the smell of oil and grease. Andrew smiled his evil smile and pointed to a darkened glass door along the side of the building. He swiped a card and the door hissed open. We entered a stairwell, and directly ahead was a shelving system with boxes like in a hotel.

"Mobile phone, thanks," Andrew said, hold-ing out his hand. "No phones to interrupt us, but importantly, no photos either. Remember the Elev-enth Commandment, Benny. Thou shalt not get caught."

I nodded, understanding his point. Wives, partners, families, clients, and the world in gen-eral loved fucking gossip. Reputations could be trashed and careers ruined with an incriminating pic or video.

We climbed two flights of stairs, and my mouth fell open as a vast space the length and width of the building was revealed, the same smoky gray one-way glass overlooking the main road giving an assurance of privacy. Polished wood floors with rugs gave the place a masculine feel. One end of the room was filled with an enormous bar, behind which several girls were serving drinks.

I recognized quite a few prominent business-men involved in everything from fast food fran-chises to motor dealerships, at least two doctors, a transport fleet operator whose home I'd sold a few months ago, several self-employed tradesmen, a retired magistrate, and, as I was told later, a cur-rent serving policeman from the middle ranks.

There were no formal introductions; first names were considered enough. But everyone knew who was who. A boys' club for sure, but with membership fees which were stupendous.

"Don't worry about it, Benny," Andrew said when I told him I simply couldn't afford to join. "This is a legitimate business expense. Smithson Real Estate picks up the tab."

Andrew waved his hand to a large curtained-off area opposite the bar, a discreet door visible to one side near the toilets. "That's the starting stalls over there," Andrew whispered. "Rooms with or with-out doors in case anyone wants to share, if you get my drift."

I understood. It was done cleverly—a trip to the toilets with a quick wink to one of the girls and it was all systems go. *How bloody boring. I can get that for free.*

I wandered around the big space. Expensive-looking chairs and lounge suites were arranged in semicircles, "hostesses" trotting around with trays of drinks and others with bowls filled with joints like candy. I sat down, intrigued at the variety of stuff available. I even saw a hookah there, the water bubbling and the smell of apple permeating the place, but obviously more than shisha tobacco was being smoked. Marijuana fumes hung in the air like a fog, and I accepted a joint from one of the girls. It was like I'd finished work a little earlier and relaxed as I'd done every night for years, peacefully smoking a joint. Soon I was laughing at the silliest of jokes, and the despair of Tammy's departure seemed far away and of no consequence. For the first time in many months, I was actually enjoying myself.

I preferred dope to alcohol, considering my father's addiction, but I enjoyed a glass of red wine occasionally. So I had a big glass, still giggling away as I washed down some beautiful finger food. By now the girls had taken off their tops and were getting felt up as they waited on the cream of our town's society. In my relaxed mindset, it occurred to me that my recent celibate state could easily come to an end if I wanted it to. One of the girls was giving me a sly smile and rolling her eyes toward the "naughty door." Against my better judgment, I followed. I was high, and I was suddenly as hard as steel. She fell to her knees, her serving tray discarded, and my pants dropped around my ankles as if by magic. After a few minutes, she paused and looked up at me. She would have been late twenties, I guessed, and quite hot, even though I already assumed they were hired from the local brothel.

"If you want to fuck me, it'll cost you extra," she said, "but blow jobs are on the house." She went straight back to work, but I was already deflating, and she lifted her head. Her lipstick had left a red ring around my dick, and that was the final straw.

"Let's give it a miss, love," I said. She scowled at me, grabbed her serving tray, and left in a huff. As I wandered back to the main room, I noticed a pair of expensive black patent-leather shoes casually left in a doorway and realized they belonged to my boss. I squinted into the dimly lit area to see his white arse pumping away while another guy looked on. I blinked as I recognized Grant Hopkins from LGP Real Estate, a regular around the cottages. As my eyes adjusted to the gloom, I noticed he wasn't watching the chick, he was watching Andrew's dick pumping away, as expected. I wasn't about to blow his cover. I had too much to hide, and I certainly wasn't interested in Andrew, the sleazy prick, so I kept walking to more interesting things.

OUT IN the main lounge area, things were heating up. The girls had disappeared, no doubt all in the back rooms at about three hundred an hour.

"Come and get geared up," one of my new friends said. "There's some cool stuff here. There's shabu over there." He pointed to a table where lines of white powder were being greedily sniffed up.

"What's that?" I whispered, not wanting to show my ignorance.

"Meth and coke," he explained. "It'll get you going, but I've got some Tina here, very pure."

"What's Tina?" I asked stupidly.

"Don't ask if you don't know, but this stuff is the best, and it's free in this place. How cool is that?"

My new friend was close to my age and introduced himself as Brett, a self-made millionaire manufacturing carbon fiber components for the automotive industry. I knew of his family. I'd sold some commercial properties for them, but I remembered Brett had left his family electrical engineering business and gone out on his own, contracted to the burgeoning Chinese automotive industry. He was courted by town hall and the state government alike, always in the news, and I wondered idly why he'd bother with me, a nobody in town, although I sensed a note of physical interest on his behalf. I decided to ignore it and go with the flow as he rolled two blunts and we fired up together, leaning back in armchairs in a quiet corner of the room.

Brett had married his high school sweetheart, and they had two kids, he told me proudly, but he liked some "… alternative action, because I can never get enough at home," he said as he grabbed the almost obscene mound between his legs.

I'd never seen him around the cottages and wondered how he kept his "alternative action" going.

"Grindr," he said. "Mostly married blokes like me."

"But that's really gay." I grinned at him, teasing him, with a most amazing sense of well-being. So much so that I felt completely in charge of everything, including him. "Why me?" I asked.

"That's easy. You're the best-looking bloke in the room."

"But I'm straight."

"Whenever did that matter? So am I, and you've got the best ass I've ever seen."

I leaned over him, full of confidence, my own secrets still intact. "No one taps my ass, Brett baby, but if you're a good little boy, you can suck my dick."

He seemed shocked that someone else was calling the shots but recovered quickly when he considered my proposition. I reckoned he would be a raver given half a chance, but for now I was in charge. He would do as he was told—simple.

"We can't do anything here," he whispered, a look of fear in his eyes. "Too dangerous. The worst kind of networking. We'd never work in this town again."

"Well, it's your call, princess. Do you want to forget about my cock and pretend it never happened?"

"Oh no, no, no," he said. "My office at the factory—I have sleeping quarters there. I'll get my driver."

Chapter 14
HOME EARLY

I WALKED in the door at 9:30 p.m., surprising even myself.

Mum raised her eyebrows. Gloria had told her that Andrew and I were attending the "boys' club" and not to expect me until late, if at all. But here I was, minus my vehicle and in a presentable condition, except I felt—different. I knew I was as high as a kite, but I felt it was something I should keep to myself. I didn't want Mum worrying, she'd had enough of that, and Peter didn't need to know his dad had enough drugs in his system to power the entire town.

I'd enjoyed myself. I had little in common with the other guys, but I'd been seen there, and according to Gloria, that was important. I'd certainly made some new contacts, smoked some amazing stuff, and surprise, surprise, the underbelly of the town was on display for those who wanted to experience it. First the hooker who hoped a sloppy blow job might lead to a bigger reward, then Grant Hopkins pretending he was so heterosexual while perving on the guys, including my boss, and finally Brett Evers, who spirited me away to his factory and gave me a blow job to remember. Blow jobs from guys were good fun. The cottage culture in the parks and reserves suggested there were many straight guys like me availing themselves of the opportunities there. I was unwilling to put labels on people, but I'd seen Grant there getting fucked on several occasions, and my new mate Brett seemed to be fascinated with cocks, suggesting I might like to plunder his bum as often as possible. I'd changed the subject without refusing him outright, which seemed to calm him down, and we settled for some more of the Tina instead.

I felt really full-on. I had a cup of tea with Mum, nearly scalding my mouth I drank it so quickly. All the while I was thinking about the auction I had tomorrow—a huge historic mansion in New Hampton, classified by the National Trust. I looked in on Peter, who was sleeping the sleep of the innocent, his hair fanned out across the pillow, and I felt even more inspired to make a name for myself. I went into my bedroom and pulled out the laptop, found all the potential customers for this type of property, and resent them emails, reminding them of the auction, the time and location.

I showered and slipped under the covers, but sleep evaded me. My mind was working beautifully; a theoretically sleepless night didn't worry me. I tossed all the scenarios around in my head, even studying the weather forecast on my phone. Finally, at around 5:00 a.m. I jumped out of bed and did something unusual for me—I went for a run. I found some old but decent-looking shorts, my nice runners, and a T-shirt, which I reckoned was the "uniform" for the physically fit locals, and set out. I found a new fitness I didn't know I had, passing several other guys and chicks with ease, feeling superior in my style and speed.

"Who's that?" I heard a girl say as I swept past, making me feel really good.

I ran in the drive, speeding up, and shot in the front door, surprising Mum, who was enjoying an early cup of tea.

"You're up early, dear," she said as I forged ahead in the direction of the bathroom.

I showered, shaved carefully, and gelled my hair so I'd look the part at the auction this afternoon at two o'clock. But it was barely seven o'clock as Mum decided to cook me breakfast. I was suddenly ravenous and ate what three people would normally put away: three eggs, bacon, tomatoes, sausages, and several rounds of toasted whole-meal bread. Mia was up and about by this time, surprising since she had a rare Saturday off from her job in retail. Timmy was up as well. They looked in awe at my breakfast, shaking their heads.

"That's enough for the entire house," Mia said, laughing, "including Garry, and he eats like a horse. I can't ever stop work with him around." Mum joined in the joke with "We might have to take out another mortgage to keep him fed."

I knew it was a joke, and I tried to join in, but words somehow escaped me, the mention of a mortgage upping my anxiety about my performance this afternoon. But something also wasn't right. I knew Garry, Mia's boyfriend, would be snoring away in Mia's bed. He spent every weekend with us and several nights during the week, so that was quite usual for him, as a shift worker. Garry had become part of the family group, someone we liked and respected, mainly because it was clear he adored my sister. He was also reliable and responsible, helping me with maintenance tasks without ever being asked.

But someone else was missing from the breakfast table, and it irritated me. I rounded on Timmy. "Where's Helen?" I demanded, quite rudely, because I never really liked her. She was a domineering, bullying influence on my brother, such a gentle little bloke who I thought deserved better.

"Gone," said Tim.

"Gone home early?" I persisted.

"No, Ben, gone for good. She didn't find me interesting enough, so we broke up."

I felt awful. Through my nosiness I could have hurt my brother's feelings, and while I was secretly happy the bitch had gone, Timmy had to move on with his life, a familiar feeling to me after the Tammy debacle. I seemed to be struggling with my emotions that morning: great anxiety and excitement over the auction, then sadness mixed with elation over Timmy's news. I jumped up and threw my arms around my baby brother while Mum watched with amusement.

"You kids live separate lives at times," Mum said, "but when there's trouble of any nature, you're as thick as thieves again." She laughed, kicked me under the table, and gave me her "talk to you later" look, a device we'd used over the years when I was the only father my siblings had known. Later came when Timmy went to his room to get dressed for work.

"It only happened this week," Mum told me, "but he wouldn't really talk about Helen at all. I think he was secretly relieved, but like most males, he keeps things to himself."

I managed to laugh at her. She was obviously referring to my fucked-up and closed mindset after Tammy and I broke up, but at least I had Peter to show from our time together. Timmy had nothing but probably bad memories of a girlfriend from his school days who liked running him down in front of as many people as she could muster so she could feel good about herself.

"Well, what do you think?" Mum said.

"Huh?" I replied, looking stupidly at her.

"I said, dear, that I've invited Kenny over. I'm sure he'll keep your brother focused like he did for you when Tammy left."

"Mum," I said, shocked and perhaps more forcefully than I should have, "you don't even know if Timmy's gay."

"Well, darling, you're not gay, but Kenny certainly helped you through a bad period, didn't he?"

I put my head down. My mother was absolutely right. Kenny had helped restore my self-esteem while no one in our home made any comment about his sleepovers. He was treated like any friend who stepped in when one of us was in trouble.

Mum studied my face as conflicting emotions swirled around in my head. "Oh dear, I didn't realize there was something still going on with you and Kenny. Should I cancel him, Benny?"

I had to laugh at last. My dear matchmaking mother was covering all the bases, not the least of which was that perhaps my baby brother might prefer a bloke in his bed.

"No, Mum, nothing like that, but Kenny has been a great friend to us all, and as I recall, he and Timmy seemed to get on well together."

"That's exactly what I thought, dear."

Chapter 15
THE UNRAVELING BEGINS

"LADIES AND gentlemen, the property is now on the market," I said with meaning as I studied the crowd. Gloria and I had researched the interested parties the day before, and nothing surprised us as we slipped past the reserve of one point five million dollars with ease, my Chinese contacts watching the crowd even more closely than I was. They'd run it up quickly to frighten off challengers, but I knew there were at least two other local bidders who had the funds to blow them off.

The lull in proceedings morphed into a long silence; I could hear the insects buzzing in the yellow flowers of the laburnum close to my head, but nothing else. My composure returned. None of the doubts that had plagued me a few hours earlier troubled me now. I felt strong, invincible, and totally in charge. This was my day, and no one was going to rain on my parade. I decided I was going to take advantage of the temporary lack of bidding to give everyone a lecture.

"This house," I roared, "is on the market for the first time in one hundred and fifty years. Are you telling me it's only worth one and a half million dollars? Well, that's only the first reserve. I'll be recommending the vendors withdraw it for sale if it doesn't reach at least double that figure." My vendors, Stan and Kathy Brown, smiled uncertainly at me but smiled nonetheless, and the crowd got the message. "If you want this magnificent property, you'll have to fight for it, because it's so unique. If you don't want it for yourself but have high hopes of stealing it at auction and on-selling it later, then forget it. You have to want this beautiful place for yourself and your family."

The Chinese blanched at my words and tried looking out to sea. Out of nowhere came a gruff voice. "Two million."

"Two point five million," called out another, a well-known business lady. Gloria turned and winked at me. Good, that meant she was cashed up and had the ego to get on with it.

"Two million six," called out another, and on it went.

To everyone's amazement, including the vendors, it ran quickly past three million and ended up being a contest between two bidders—Angela Murray, the businesswoman, and Craig Evers, Brett's younger brother. Craig wasn't anything like Brett, and I sensed that Daddy had probably sent him to buy the house to get him out of the way. He made a phone call, nodded, and despite my taking ten-thousand-dollar bids, Angela Murray stepped in with yet another one hundred thousand, and I knocked it down to her for four million two hundred thousand dollars.

"Sold," I yelled, and the crowd went ballistic.

We signed everything up, took a gigantic deposit, and I helped the vendors stick the Sold sign on the board. I turned and walked back to the car, feeling drained, even a little depressed. Saturday night was coming up, and I had nowhere to go, no one to share my huge success with except my family. I was a little sad as well, and tired. I reasoned I hadn't slept well last night, so no wonder I felt secondhand. My limbs began to ache as if I had a dose of the flu or something similar, and I had this raging thirst. Perhaps a beer would be in order.

Everyone was out. I texted Peter, who was at a school function with Mia and Garry. They had unselfishly stepped into my shoes on their weekend off. Tim was taking a few days annual leave. As Mum had suggested, he was hanging with Kenny—surprise, surprise. Mum was working night shift. It was late afternoon, so I thought, *fuck it, I'm tired, but I dare not try for a nap or I won't sleep properly again tonight. I'll have a smoke instead and hopefully feel better. My aches and pains are killing me.* I found my stash and fired up, and after a few minutes I felt quite mellow. My phone beeped with a text, and it was Brett Evers.

U want to hang out at the factory?

Why not, I replied. *Some of your good stuff might help me feel better than I do now.*

The Evers family looked after themselves very nicely, I decided as Brett's driver pulled into the driveway in a nondescript dark gray BMW. I

realized in this set, BMWs were like arseholes—
everyone had one, even me. But the Evers mob
seemed to go about their business quietly; the car
fitted in perfectly with their image. It could quite
easily have been a hire car, but it wasn't, and "call
me Jake," the driver, was clearly on the Evers pay-
roll, probably with a huge salary, not only to drive
the family members from one risqué address to
another but to keep his mouth shut at all times.

When we reached the factory, Brett opened
the door and ushered me inside. "Rough day?" he
asked.

"Biggest auction of my career, with a stupendous price," I said.

"So I heard. We got blown off when it hit four
mil. You must be stoked."

"Well, I'm pleased, but I'm still wound up like
a spring, and I feel like shit."

Brett reached for my zipper, and I didn't stop
him. I came quickly, but my headache increased,
which was unusual. Sex normally relaxed me. It
wasn't until a grinning Brett lit up a joint laced
with Tina that my system autocorrected almost instantly. We lay back on the settee, my pants around
my ankles and Brett with his mouth over my dick,
trying to encourage it back to life. It wasn't working very well for him or me, so I suggested we
smoke a little more. My phone screamed, and I
turned the speaker on so Brett Evers knew I was
more important than some nobody he'd picked up
for his own pleasure.

"You coming home for tea?" Mia asked.

"No, leave something for me."

"But Peter hasn't seen you for nearly two days. He's asking for his Dad."

"Look, I'm not everyone's wet shoulder, Mia. I'm fucking stressed, do you hear? I'll get home when I can."

Chapter 16
IGNORING THE SIGNPOSTS

I SWEPT into work Monday morning to a subdued welcome, thinking my very public success would be reflected in a nice morning tea for us all at the very least. Instead my boss had a face like a ruptured arsehole, spoke to no one, signed a few checks, and left late morning "… for parts unknown," said Gloria.

"What's up his clacker?" I asked.

"He's jealous of you, Benny," she said. "Insanely jealous. It's been so obvious lately. He thought auctioning the Brown's property at the weekend was madness, that it should've been for private sale, but you blew his judgment out the window again. Once more you were right and he was wrong. Results like that are showing he's out of touch."

"But what about the commission, for Christ's sake. He's making a fortune."

"His ego drives him, Benny, simple as that. But I also think something else is bothering him. He's behaving very strangely, and I keep fielding calls from his wife, trying to find him. He hasn't been home since Friday morning."

I wondered about Andrew; we'd seen a lot less of him since he'd made me sales manager, with Phillip and Amanda reporting to me and Gloria, as usual, doing everything else. He was fine when we fronted up together at his club on Friday afternoon. I even told him I was leaving early with Brett Evers, and that actually seemed to make him happy. So why had he gotten so shitty with everyone so quickly, particularly me, and where the fuck had he been since Friday?

Gloria motioned me into her office and closed the door. "I've got Pam on the line again," she said. "I'll put her on speaker."

"Pam?"

"His missus."

"Oh, Gloria, he's walked in," Pam said. "Thank heavens. Must have been a good boys' party on Friday. He evidently met up with some old school friends, and they've been partying ever since. As usual I'm the last to know, but this will cost him dearly. I hope you're having a good month?"

Gloria grinned evilly at me. "Yes, Pam, a really good month, thanks to our Ben. What about a nice cruise? The place runs better with him out of it."

"Why would I take *him*?" she said, spitting the words out like bullets. "He can stay home and look after the kids. Then he might begin to understand what hard work's all about."

ACCORDING TO Andrew, the chip on my shoulder was the reason he'd employed me in the first place, and up until this week, he was probably right in that respect. I'd always been trying to prove something. I was highly competitive, taking delight in pinching listings from other agencies, and I'd walked over the top of others as I lined my pockets with cash. I made sure my profile was uppermost in the local press, including the report on Saturday's auction, where the reporter claimed I was "Mr. Magic of Real Estate" and a future leader in the business sector in our town. All of it good stuff, feeding my ego. But since the weekend I'd felt quite different, as if all my insecurities had vanished. Flashbacks to where I felt inadequate or embarrassed weren't happening anymore, and I was complete at last, my own man.

I decided to spread the cheer a little bit, showing Phillip and Amanda I wasn't a prick all the time and that we were all on the same team together, so I took them to the Italian restaurant next door for coffee.

"This is really nice," Amanda said.

Phillip nodded. "That's right. It's not always about the money, and a bit of time spent together is really good. There's lots of things we never get to talk about."

"Such as?" I asked.

"Well, our boss, for one thing," Amanda said. "We hardly see him these days, and when we do, he's not on our wavelength."

"I doubt if that'll alter," I said. "And on that basis, I guess we should have a little sales meeting of our own, say every Monday morning at eight o'clock. How does that sound?"

They beamed back at me. Andrew had recruited them in a similar fashion to me. Neither had a real-estate background. Amanda had been a waitress and Phillip a trades advisor at Bunnings. Both had a similar induction into Smithson Real Estate; they were thrown to the wolves and allowed to fend for themselves. Gloria and I were alarmed at the risk they posed to the business, because they could so easily get into real trouble, financial or legal, without some basic training, and we could all be looking for employment. It was common sense to review each and every sale to ensure all bases were covered, four sets of eyes and ears looking for mistakes, creating a learning curve for us all. Andrew continued to drive around in his Jaguar, and it seemed, without his verbalizing the fact, that he expected me to run the place, only getting involved when one of us fucked up, or when he thought I'd made a really bad decision, like auctioning the Brown property at the weekend.

WEDNESDAY CAME around. I seemed to catch up on my sleep, but things at home were, for once, less than perfect. It seemed my outburst on the phone at my sister at the weekend had gone down like a lead balloon. Even Mum seemed pissed off. Even worse, my son tried to studiously avoid me until I demanded he tell me what was wrong.

"It's you, Dad." He sniffled. "You've been *horrible*," he said, with enough emphasis to sting.

I didn't argue. What was the point? They were clearly all talking about me behind my back, and

I knew I'd have to be extremely careful if I was to avoid criticism in the future. I could tell they were talking about me because every time I walked into the kitchen, the conversation would die down and Mum would look strangely at me.

"You all right, dear?" she asked as I picked at my breakfast, trying to focus on what was ahead of me for the day.

"Yes. I feel as if I have the flu coming on," I said. "Aches in my joints, and my head is splitting again." I sat there while she took my temperature, seething with the indignity of being treated like a child but terrified of her diagnostic skills.

I rang Brett midmorning, and although he sounded busy, he was pleased to hear from me, unlike some people. "You doing anything tonight?" I asked. "I could do with a hit of Tina."

"Ben, that's for the weekend, and even then, not every weekend. I have to take my kids camping next weekend, and tonight it's dinner with my wife's parents."

"Oh, okay," I said, feeling a little paranoid, like my options were slipping away and no one seemed interested in me anymore. "So where can I score some?"

There was hesitation at the other end. "Hang on," he said, and there followed the sound of a door closing. "Benny boy," he said, which infuriated me because I was supposed to be in charge, "you have to be careful with that stuff. Tina is crystal meth, you know, and it's not to be taken lightly. Last weekend was great, but if you make it a regular habit, it could fuck you up very easily."

"I'm not stupid, Brett *baby*," I shot back, "but I need some for a standby. Who do I talk to?"

"You know Brendan Street, Cranmere?"

"Ah yeah, it runs behind the cop shop."

"Correct. Enter from the highway end and keep going until you see a park on the right-hand side. Be there at 3:30 p.m. sharp and wait for the drug bus."

I thought this sounded like the greatest joke I'd ever heard but decided I'd nothing to lose anyway. Cranmere had a dreadful reputation; we usually refused to sell property there because of its socioeconomic disaster base, high unemployment, and the worst crime rate in the state, the place awash with drugs. I sat in the BMW and noticed a few other nice cars nearby. Suddenly a high-roof converted bus with its windows blanked out drove quietly down the street and parked discreetly away from the park entrance. To my amazement, doors flew open up and down the street as women in dressing gowns, people in wheelchairs, and nursing mothers mixed in with business types like me. It was like a food van at the market; there was a temporary counter across the door opening, people knew what they wanted, and they bought their stuff and scurried away almost as quickly as they'd appeared. When I asked for meth, the only question was "Do you want top shelf?"

"Tina," I said, and was surprised how inexpensive it was compared to a few nice bottles of wine. Within minutes I was back at the office, my stash secured, feeling a sense of achievement, knowing I would be in better shape than ever tomorrow.

First, however, I had to set things right at home. I knew I wasn't the most popular bloke these days, so I phoned Mum.

"Don't cook tonight," I said. "We'll get Uber Eats. I'll have a stupendous pay packet this month."

"Okay, dear, but I suggest you buy a gift for Mia and Garry. They've kept the home fires burning while I've been on night shift, and poor little Peter—you've hardly paid him any attention lately."

I hung my head. I knew I'd been a prick, but my family had to understand I'd finally left a difficult life behind me, and if I needed some time for myself they'd have to be more understanding in the future. I prepared some of my little parcel quietly. My new dealer had shown me how to get quality stuff into me quickly, and after some initial needle sticks, I got the stuff flowing through my system, taking care to dispose of the evidence afterward. It worked faster this way; like a tsunami it swept over me, the earlier lethargy, joint pain, and headache disappearing instantly. I was wired, could have led an army into battle, knowing they would follow me to the ends of the earth. But I also knew my family would never believe this new "me" and would continue to have doubts about my abilities. It was vital they knew nothing about this; they couldn't possibly understand how I'd matured with such lightning speed, so I had to play my cards close to my chest.

Chapter 17
A SHOCK TO THE SYSTEM

GLORIA WAS watching me, I knew, but her concern was simply on a personal level; in her eyes I had to be the leader of our little group because our boss was always missing in action. In the meantime, we put some figures on the board that were stupendous. The market was problematic because interest rates had risen slightly, and prospective clients were being... careful. The secret of our success was a realistic asking price, refusing to list stuff that was overpriced for the times, and turning our Chinese friends on like nothing else, people who knew a bargain when they saw one. I told Amanda and Phillip how competent and professional they'd been. Three months into the "downturn," the three of us together, with support from Gloria, had managed a month that was the best on record for Smithson Real Estate.

On the first Monday morning of the new month, I decided to start the sales meeting at 7:30 a.m. and buy everyone a nice big breakfast at the restaurant next door to celebrate. We had a big long table in a semiprivate part at the rear and were on our second coffee when there was shouting from the direction of the register. Andrew strode up to our table. "What are you people doing here?" he screamed. "There's work to be done, and that doesn't include sitting on your asses drinking fucking coffee on my time."

"Andrew," Gloria said calmly, "we've finished our sales meeting, the one you were invited to and had the rudeness not to acknowledge. Smithson Real Estate has completed an all-time record month in both volume and profitability, and Ben decided we'd buy everyone breakfast as a reward for their hard work."

"What fucking bullshit," he screamed. "I ought to sack all of you. Some lovely old established agents in town will be closing their doors soon unless we stop taking business away from them, a tragedy in this industry. I can tell you there's going to be some administrative changes around here. Watch this space." He pivoted on his heels and stomped out of the place as we turned and looked at each other.

"Let's have another coffee," Gloria said, "and plan the rest of our working lives, because I think our Andy Pandy has lost it completely."

Amanda and Phillip were close to tears, and I felt so remorseful. Fancy being chastised for being successful!

"Guys," I said, "Gloria and I have always talked about opening our own agency. In fact we've threatened Andrew with that possibility."

"Makes me feel a little better," Phillip said, and Amanda nodded in agreement.

"What we need, however, before we make a move, is to have a franchise," I said. "That's where the big money is because the marketing spend and exposure is guaranteed. So if you're patient with us, we'd include you guys in the new business."

"You'd still want us?" Amanda said.

"Of course," Gloria snapped. "You guys are the best in this business. You take direction well, you listen to us, and you contribute to our strategy as a group, besides being great salespeople. Take no notice of Andy. I think he has some personal problems."

Chapter 18
A PARTING OF THE WAYS

I NOTICED my teeth, particularly my gums, were sore all the time, and every day they seemed worse. Then my teeth seemed stained, and I freaked out. The final straw was when a sore appeared on my face; nothing like this had happened since puberty, and it looked gross. I complained to Mum, who looked at me through worried eyes.

"Are you run down, dear?" she said. "Perhaps you need a little break." She was quiet for a while, ominous for Mum because it meant her mind was processing medical knowledge while she sipped her second coffee. Her eyes narrowed. "Show me your teeth again. What are you on, Ben, to stain your beautiful teeth like that?"

"N-nothing," I said. "Only a bit of dope every now and then."

"I want you to see Eddie Chan," she said. "In my opinion he's the most competent GP at the hospital, as well as specializing in infectious diseases. You may have picked up something nasty. And you've been so irritable here at home, almost like your mind is playing tricks on you. Make the appointment now. You need to hit this on the head. It spoils your appearance, and you need everything going for you in your job."

Not to do as Mum ordered in matters of health in particular would be sudden death for me. I'd lose all her support at home, branded a pariah if I didn't toe the line.

Dr. Chan was a pleasant little bloke, his Chinese ancestry showing through in his manners and courtesy. On the second visit, we discussed my tests, and then he turned my folder face down on his desk. "With respect, Ben, this is all pointless, isn't it? You have no infectious diseases, but you do have, I suspect, a methamphetamine habit which has taken over your life."

I stood up in his office, angry beyond belief. "How dare you," I hissed, all appreciation for Dr. Chan's manners and Asian charm lost in my outrage. "I have a few tokes every now and then. I'm no junkie."

"Then what are the needle marks on your inside elbow?" he said quietly. "Only when you become the subject of police action, and that, sadly, is inevitable, will I consider giving your mother my professional opinion. Until then I feel bound by my Hippocratic oath, so this is between us for the time being."

I lost it. This sanctimonious bastard was intent on ruining my reputation and my career, and I tore out of his office. From nowhere security appeared, and I knew they were all in the fucking plot to discredit me. I swung a punch and found myself on the floor in the foyer, looking into the eyes of a huge, ugly guard whose breath smelled of garlic.

"Now, pretty boy," he said, "it's your choice. Walk out of here like a gentleman with the intention of not returning in the near future, or I call the coppers."

I remembered what the doctor had said and couldn't stand the risk of Mum getting involved in my problems, so I nodded. A small crowd gathered around. The last thing I needed was that sort of publicity, so I moved out quickly, found the Beemer, and drove home.

Mum was there, waiting expectantly. "Well, dear, what did Eddie have to say?"

"Oh, nothing much. I do have a slight hormonal imbalance, which has caused the skin rash and the sore gums, but apart from that I'm pretty fit."

Mum didn't buy it, I knew, but at least I'd done as she'd asked.

THANK HEAVENS I had something to fall back on. My life had become immensely better since Tina became my friend. She was worth the few ups and downs. After all, I was a runaway success in my career, and I was well-known and admired in business, which unfortunately now seemed to irritate Andrew Smithson, but who gave a fuck anyway. Tina was never wrong. I thought I was imagining things at times, but she let me know when people were talking about me. She was there when I needed her.

Perhaps I'd been a bit careless; regular use often left little telltale signs. But I knew I could do anything. My sex life was almost entirely by myself; I found I liked masturbating without the complication of other people. Sometimes on my one weekend a month off, I'd come home Friday night, catch up with my son and the rest of the family, and then get with Tina. I never slept but locked the door and indulged myself in some wild times, sometimes watching porn, sometimes enjoying the technicolor world of crystal meth, with some amazing fantasies which were totally real for me without any responsibility for anyone else.

I could trace the deterioration of my relationship with Andrew Smithson back to that Friday afternoon at the Business Club, but I couldn't work out why. I'd gone from hero to zero from that day onward. Something gnawed at my subconscious level, but I couldn't figure out why that day had changed his attitude toward me so profoundly. I'd told him I was leaving with Brett Evers, and he'd seemed delighted. It must have been clear I'd been enjoying some drugs like he had. So what was it? Tina was a help in these matters at times; I seemed to have a sixth sense now, and I remembered Andrew screwing one of the escort girls. Perhaps that was behind his mindset. I'd naturally said nothing of what went on behind closed doors, but Andrew's relationship with Pam, his wife, seemed very rocky since that day, so maybe he'd been seeing the hooker since?

I WAS actually running late for the sales meeting the following Monday morning after taking Peter to school. I walked into the room, and my hair stood on end; something wasn't right. There, center stage, sitting next to Andrew, was Grant Hopkins, the "'queen of the cottages," from LGP Real Estate.

"Well, good afternoon," Andrew said sarcastically. "So nice of you to grace us with your presence."

I stood there while Gloria, Phillip, and Amanda looked on, obviously as confused as I was.

"Well," Andrew barked, "where's your agenda? I've not bothered attending these meetings much." He turned to Grant, who was grinning like an idiot. "They never seemed to discuss anything worthwhile."

"But that's not the case, Andy Pandy." Gloria smiled. "If it wasn't your idea, then you were never interested anyway. This is the agenda Ben gave me on Friday, and Amanda has added to it since, so don't get fucking smart with me." Gloria pressed a button and the neatly typed order of business was projected onto the wall.

Grant Hopkins went pale; whatever the reason for his presence at our meeting, it was clear he hadn't expected his friend Andrew to be held in such low esteem in his own business.

I finally found my voice. Tina was screaming inside my head, but I was still confused as to why a member of an opposition real estate company would be sitting in on our meeting, where we'd be reviewing every piece of business we were working and, importantly, everything we'd hoped to sign up that week.

"Why is he here?" I said bluntly, pointing at Grant.

"That's easy." Andrew smiled. "He's the new sales manager of Smithson Real Estate. You'll be utilized as a salesman"—he waved his hand at Phillip and Amanda—"along with these two."

Blood ran to my face as Andrew and Grant smirked at me. Somehow I managed to keep my cool. Tina told me not to let go until I was properly prepared.

Gloria stood. "Ben, Amanda, Phillip, office," she said, pointing to the door. "Clean out your desks."

Andrew started shouting, and Grant looked confused. Ten minutes later we were next door at the restaurant while Andrew screamed profanities from the footpath.

"I've been expecting this ," she said, "but don't worry, you're not out of work. I've had a company name registered as Gloria Dixon Real Estate, and one of our clients has a lovely little office available not two hundred meters away. Ben, you and I talked about this, and we threatened the prick if he didn't behave, but now he's crossed the line. He and Grant Hopkins are having a dirty little affair, using vacant rental properties for their trysts, sometimes even spending the night at the Regal Hotel, where they've been known to host orgies."

"But Andrew's a married man. I've met Pam, and she's lovely," said Amanda, close to tears.

"And Mr. Hopkins is also a married man," Gloria said and smiled, "but when did that ever matter to people like that?"

Phillip was shaking his head in disbelief, no doubt worrying about his wife and three-month-old baby at home. I sat there, quietly furious, Tina pointing in the direction of the office of my former employer with an anger that was palpable. I thought of the long days, the weekends without a break, working for Andrew Smithson. Yes, Andrew had generally picked his staff from lowly occupations and grown them into high producers, but I'd more than doubled the turnover with help from Gloria and now Amanda and Phillip. But this wasn't about them. It was a personal slight against me, and I felt the immense hurt and selfishness of Andrew Smithson invade my senses. I couldn't care less who he was fucking, but he'd clearly known for months what he wanted to do to keep his new boyfriend happy, while pretending he and Grant were lovely, holier-than-thou family men. Tina and I were in agreement; this disloyalty to me, my mates, and their own families would not go unpunished.

Gloria laid her hand on my arm as my feelings of indignation took hold like a cancer. "Ben," she said, "I know it's hard, but don't let the bastard get to you. Let's get the new place humming along and take all his business from him—it couldn't happen to a nicer prick. He's shown us his true colors, as I thought he would. Admittedly in a different way, but that's Andrew."

I nodded and smiled at Gloria. She'd been a great ally, and our friendship had deepened after Tammy departed, our professional relationship carrying us along as a successful team. Tina's voice was shrill now, but I was calm and determined.

"Toilet," I said and moved toward the rear of the restaurant. I walked out into the car park, stepped deliberately into the Beemer, and gunned up the diesel with a roar. I backed out of my slot and drove around the front of the office. Through the door I could see Andrew and Grant behind Gloria's desk, smiling at each other like a pair of sickos. I selected low gear and gunned the engine. The Beemer jumped the curb with a roar, and glass and aluminum exploded around us. The last thing I remember was the look on Grant Hopkins's face, and it wasn't one of satisfaction like I'd seen after he'd sucked off someone at the cottages. I also heard Andrew Smithson screaming, which was wonderful, and then everything went blank.

Chapter 19
IN DEEP SHIT

I WAS struggling. I seemed to be emerging from a deep sleep, but it wasn't my bed. It had shiny metal rails, and the bottom sheet was a different color. I found I couldn't move; I seemed to be tied down somehow. Blood was trickling down my cheek. I could taste it, and it smeared my chest as I moved my head, the only part of me that seemed mobile. I looked to the side, and Mum was there. She held my hand and put her fingers over her lips.

"Rest, love," she said and then called out to someone as Eddie Chan appeared around the corner.

"Ah, Ben, you're with us," he said. "Feel a bit groggy?"

"Why am I tied down?" I yelled. "Let me up, let me out of this place."

"Not possible at the moment, Ben," Eddie said. "Do you remember how you got here?"

"Get fucked," I screamed. "Let me up. I've got to go back to work."

A shadow blocked the light as someone else walked into the room. "Is he conscious?" this big bloke in a suit asked. Blind Freddie could see he was a copper—all balls, no brains. "Benjamin John O'Connor, I'm arresting you on grounds of attempted murder of Andrew Smithson and Grant Hopkins. I must caution you that anything you say or do may be taken down in evidence and used against you." He paused for a moment. "There'll be an armed guard outside your room twenty-four hours a day, every day, until your health has improved enough for you to be transferred to the police cells at the station. There you'll be formally charged and held in custody. We will oppose bail because we consider you to be a danger to the community." He snapped out the last sentence and walked out, leaving Mum quietly sniffling into her handkerchief.

"What happened?" I asked. Tina was nowhere around, and I desperately needed some soothing help. Eddie and Mum sat together, sorrow etched on their faces.

"You had a psychotic event, Ben, after Andrew Smithson replaced you at work with a fellow called Grant Hopkins. You deliberately drove your vehicle through the front of the premises, breaking Mr. Hopkins's foot and Mr. Smithson's left hip and some of his ribs. Both of them are listed as satisfactory, thank heavens, while you have a few nasty deep cuts and bruises."

I sort of remembered what had happened, but I wanted out of there. "Let me up, for Christ's fucking sake," I roared, and my own mother slapped my face.

"Don't you dare use language like that in front of me," Mum said, and for the first time in ages I felt really frightened and started to sob.

Eddie emptied a syringe into the tubing of the IV in my arm.

"What's that?" Mum asked him.

"More ketamine," Eddie said. "It'll be a while before he's lucid enough to hold a rational conversation."

Chapter 20
FUCKED AND FAR FROM HOME

I FINALLY awoke from the cocktail of drugs in my system, was stitched up and treated for the severe bruising I'd given myself. Eddie Chan and Mum were never far away as I started coming down from the stuff in my system. I screamed my head off with the pain of withdrawal. Tina appeared to me many times, a look of disapproval and hatred in her eyes. Where she was once my savior, she was now my enemy. I was convinced she had brought a bunch of people to kill me, and I sweated and writhed around, trying to avoid the knives they were aiming at my stomach.

Every now and then, Eddie would hover over me, I'd feel a prick in my arm, and I'd go off to a dreamless sleep again. I had no idea how long I'd been in hospital, but I woke early one morning, feeling a little better, with Mum at my side.

"Ben," she said, "there are two people waiting outside I want you to meet before they cart you off to the police station."

I stared at her as if she were balmy; everyone was overreacting to all this shit, and to be honest, I only had a vague recollection of what all the fuss was about.

"Ben, dear," she said severely, which got my attention, and I knew I was toast unless I went along with whatever she had in mind.

"Unless you cooperate with these people, you could go to jail for a very long period," Mum continued. "I know both of these gentlemen from my high school days. Lewis Ferguson is a barrister, and the other is Professor Jamie Weiss, who heads up the state government drug rehabilitation program here in Victoria. You're going to need both of them—Jamie to design and implement a rehab program immediately, which will hopefully return you to a normal lifestyle, and Lewis to sweet-talk the bail justice to allow you to avoid custody, until your trial at least."

What could I do but nod?

Mum went to the door. "Come in, boys," she said, and the two blokes walked into the room. Lewis Ferguson looked permanently youthful in a tee and jeans, very unlike a legal person. The professor was more imposing but wore a friendly expression on his face that probably endeared him to most people.

"I think you should go first, Jamie," Lewis said. "After all, the defense case will rest on Ben being in your care with a rehab plan already in place—if we have no plan, we have no real defense and a possible fifteen years in jail."

"Correct," Jamie said. "Ben, sadly you're an addict with what I suspect is an ongoing psychosis caused by your administering large and consistent doses of crystal meth."

I sat bolt upright in bed and shouted at the prick. The door opened, and a young copper stuck his head in. "Everything okay, Mrs. O'Connor?" he asked.

"Thank you, Brian. He's a bit emotional until we get the stuff out of his system."

"No worries. Call out if you need me."

"Listen, you," I said, "what's wrong with having a bit of fun occasionally? I've only been using small amounts at weekends."

"No, Ben," Jamie said. "I have a list here of the amounts you've been buying from the drug bus, and that's prodigious. You've got a stash at home, which we found, and you've got tracks on both arms where you've been shooting up."

I was appalled. "Look," I said, "it's a modern world with modern pressures. I take enough to get me through the working day. I know lots of people who take more than me, and they seem to breeze along without any problems."

I watched as Professor Weiss pursed his lips, any hint of friendliness suddenly absent from his face. "Ben, your attitude is still being driven by psychosis. You have to focus on the fact that your mind is still that of an addict. The reality of your situation as a human being is quite different to your opinions regarding crystal meth."

Lewis Ferguson cut in. "What Jamie is telling you, Ben, is that unless we can convince you to present yourself to the bail justice as someone who has enthusiastically embraced rehabilitation, your life will be ruined, simple. You'll go to jail for a long period, then probably start using again on your release. So we need your cooperation to willingly submit yourself to rehab initially, and then when your trial comes up in a few months, we need to demonstrate your progress toward permanent sobriety."

Jamie Weiss looked at me, I thought, with some compassion. My mind whirled as I tried to find the real me in what I was beginning to understand was a complete mess. When a tear rolled down Mum's cheek, I caved. I thought back to when Dad had left us and how she and I had worked together to raise my brother and sister, and later on, Peter. God only knows what he would think with his father in prison. I thought for a moment. Then I felt Tina trying to reassert herself, and I told Jamie about my secret relationship with Tina.

"You're still very much coming down from the drug, and you can expect episodes like that, Ben. Don't internalize it. You were one of the unlucky ones who became addicted after your very first hit of that stuff. Your path was set out for you. It's a wicked drug, and the effects drove you to live your life out of character, with the aggressiveness and false sense of confidence which sadly is so typical. We want to help you. We want to help Mary," he said, pointing to Mum. "Will you help us?"

I nodded and tears ran down my face for the first time in ages. Mum squeezed my hand, and both Jamie and Lewis smiled at me as if I'd presented them with an expensive gift.

I found out later that Eddie Chan, on advice from Jamie Weiss, wouldn't release me to the police until nearly a week later, making a whole ten days between the incident at Smithson Real Estate and my appearance in front of Mr. Hocking, the bail justice.

Unbeknown to me, Lewis Ferguson had been hard at work with the police, and the charges were downgraded from attempted murder to dangerous driving causing injury. On that basis, Lewis assured the coppers, I'd plead guilty through mitigating circumstances. Afterward, one of the police was overheard to say that it was a pity I hadn't gotten more speed up when I hit the building and taken Smithson right out, the arsehole. It appeared my ex-boss had a terrible name for nasty deals on matters other than real estate, and he'd be battling for sympathy anywhere.

Mr. Hocking was a middle-aged man with an incisive wit, which I found surprising, but when he began speaking, it was clear he'd been briefed on all facets of the case. The police prosecutor stood up, reiterating that the original charges had been downgraded, causing Mr. Hocking to roll his eyes.

"Thank you, but I can read," he said. "Now I understand the accused, Benjamin O'Connor, will be wholly in the care of Jamie Weiss, is that correct?"

"Yes, Your Honor," Jamie said, rising to his feet.

"Ah, there you are, Professor," Mr. Hocking said. "It seems highly unusual for you to be involved in this case in such a personal manner. Please explain?"

"Well, I was approached by Ben's mother, Mary O'Connor, an old school friend. She was horrified that her son, who had supported the entire family after the breakdown of her marriage and then had made good in his career, could possibly face a lengthy prison term without proper rehabilitation, thereby ruining his life. As you know, ice is a dreadful drug. Ben was one of the unlucky people who was instantly addicted after his very first experience."

"I understand. Now are you prepared to take absolute and complete responsibility for Mr. O'Connor, and what will that mean?"

"Yes. Ben will be confined at the Waratah Centre. He will not be allowed outside at any stage until further consultation with the police and yourself. I have no idea how long it will take to rid his system of the drug, but I suspect he will stay as a guest at Waratah until his case is brought to trial."

Mr. Hocking looked over at the police prosecutor. "I take it you people will not oppose bail under these circumstances?"

"No, you honor, we support the granting of bail under these circumstances."

Mr. Hocking turned to me. "Ben," he said, " I know your brain is probably still pickled with the stuff you've been taking, but are you aware of the good intentions of your family and Professor Weiss, who have thrown you a lifeline?"

I knew enough that I'd never be compromised by Tina again, and the thought of Mum crying pushed me along to where I should be.

"Yes, Your Honor. Thank you. I know I've been given another chance, and it's appreciated. I'll try my best to get well again as soon as I can. I hope one day my family and my son will look back at this time and understand I did it for them as well as for myself."

I didn't realize until sometime later that Mr. Hocking was blown away by my remarks. He smiled at Mum as he said, "Very well, bail is set at fifteen thousand dollars. Good luck."

Chapter 21
WARATAH CENTRE

LIFE AT the Waratah Centre was all very structured—learning early recovery skills, relapse prevention, even educating my family on what to expect when I was eventually released from a probable prison term. Much of the stuff was group learning, but because we're all different with different backgrounds and on different drugs, there was as much individual attention as the limited number of therapists allowed.

One day seemed to flow into another, but there were obvious physical improvements. My teeth and gums healed, as did my complexion. My appetite returned partially. I wasn't criticized for not eating so much. Instead Jamie Weiss showed me the way to the gym, an integral part of Waratah's rehab program. I spent hours in there, which helped me physically and also countered the boredom. But there were days and nights where I had images crowding my brain, tormenting me, making me feel a craving for one hit of meth. The nights were worse because there was only night staff on duty. One such night I found myself plotting to grab the keys, get outside, and get myself a hit, but the nurse second-guessed me and led me back to bed, knocking me out with something. Jamie Weiss came in the next morning, and before he opened his mouth, I blurted out my attempted indiscretion and burst into tears.

"This is all too hard," I sobbed. "There has to be an easier way."

I was lying back on the bed, propped up on the pillows, and caught a pair of twinkling blue eyes staring deep into mine.

"Ben, you can only judge your progress from one event to another currently, which is understandable. But what I see is a brave young man who has diligently applied himself to becoming well again. I think it's time you had some visitors to buck you up and get your feet on the ground. Next Saturday afternoon your entire family will be visiting, so you have something to look forward to and something to aim for. They can see for themselves how much you've already recovered."

"Thanks," I said. "I'll be on my best behavior. Can I ask you something?"

"Certainly."

"How come you, Mum, and Lewis Ferguson were close at high school, yet we never saw anything of you guys when we kids were growing up?"

Jamie laughed, his kind face allowing some dimples to make their presence known. "Well, the three of us were great mates. Your mum and me were an item for a while, and we both looked out for Lewis, because he's a gay man and some of the arseholes at school made it hard for him. Your mum caught several of them trying to belt the bejesus out of Lewis, and she took two of them out with a right cross and a great kick to the balls. Then the teachers arrived, but those guys got the message and never tried that shit again."

I was aware my mouth was hanging open, and he laughed at me, such a gentle sound, and I felt better about the world for a short time.

"The reason Lewis and I never had much contact over the years was that Mary married your father, and as you know he was insanely jealous."

"You could have been my father." I grinned.

"One of those things." Jamie smiled. "I married an Asian girl, and we had three kids, but she went on to bigger and brighter things, left me to raise them on my own."

"I'm so sorry. I shouldn't be so nosy."

"Not at all. Life goes on, but when Mary put her hand up, we simply had to respond. You see, your efforts to step into the breadwinner's shoes didn't go unnoticed, so we felt obligated to help."

He paused, and I flew off the bed and hugged the man, vowing in my poor sick brain to try even harder to get well again.

Chapter 22
FLATLINING

IT WAS amazing to have everyone around me again, with all of them trying to talk at once. Mum sat quietly on an armchair in the corner while Peter tried to get as close a possible, arms around me, head on my shoulder. I tried to transmit some of the love to my son that he'd clearly missed for a long while. I knew it wouldn't happen overnight, and we'd need some together time to catch up where I'd left off being a parent and focused on my own selfish needs. He knew it too, his articulate little self telling everyone to go easy on me. He'd studied the effect of crystal meth on the brain and was streets in front of me, the patient/ex-addict!

Mia looked wonderful, as did Garry. They assured me they were staying put, even though they were saving for their own home. Garry had taken over all the maintenance jobs at home in my absence, and I thanked him. Clearly Mia had found her match; they seemed to fit together like a jigsaw puzzle.

As did Timmy and Kenny. With Kenny's parents working in China much of the time, they'd moved into Kenny's place. I'd never seen either of them so happy. Timmy was his normal gentle, jolly self, full of love and kindness for everyone around him, and Kenny was a changed person. In his younger days, Kenny was hard to pin down. One moment he'd be giving head jobs in the cottages and the next looking like butter wouldn't melt in his mouth. Yet now he sat quietly with my brother, even holding his hand, with a happy, goofy look on his face, and I had to pinch myself that it was the same person. Like Mia and Garry, they'd found their life partner—while I'd been fucking about on the road to ruination.

THE FOLLOWING morning, I had a visit from Jamie Weiss.

"You must have responsibilities all over Victoria," I said, "yet every time I look up, you're walking in my door."

"Delegation," he said, smiling. "That's how I get to spend time with my favorite patient."

He seemed to be appraising me as he sat there in the chair while I hauled myself up on the bed again. "How do you think you're progressing, Ben? Be honest with me."

I thought I knew what he was getting at, so I let it all hang out. "I feel much, much better physically, and it's a joy to savor those changes and improvements, but I feel there's not much excitement in my life now. It seems mundane and ordinary and at times even boring, and that's not what I was about before I fucked up on ice."

"Yes," Jamie said, nodding. "This is quite common. In my terms I call it flatlining—with apologies to parts of the medical profession where it means something else! Your brain in particular has been schooled by the drug to expect rampant highs and lows, so there's no plateau anymore where you feel moderately happy or even moderately sad. For want of a more clinical interpretation, the drug has destroyed your neural pathways where you can feel good about yourself and appreciate what it means to be happy again."

My spirits dropped, because every single thing Jamie referred to was exactly how I was at the moment. "Mate, will I ever get better completely, or am I fucked, a bloody unemotional zombie unable to enjoy life and, worse, still making life a misery for those around me?"

Jamie looked at me sharply, worry etched on his face. "Our experience has been that it takes around two years, with lots of therapy, to get people back to somewhere near their old selves. But there is a method that is proving to have most encouraging improvements in patients like yourself, in a much-reduced time frame. It's like a finishing school—in Thailand."

I stared at him. As much as I liked and trusted Jamie, here I was, a hophead out on bail—no job, no income, and probably a jail sentence hanging over my head. Once I was away from the Waratah Centre, I guessed I might not see my own bed again for up to five years or so, my immediate future out of my control completely, yet he was talking about going to bloody Thailand. I wasn't a complete moron; I'd heard the Thais had several advanced rehab centers producing amazing results. The money alone frightened the shit out of me. Mum seemed to be spending a fortune on me, which was totally unfair on her.

There was a knock on the door, and in walked Mum with Lewis Ferguson, chattering away like two old sheilas.

"Morning, dear," Mum said, coming over and kissing my cheek.

"Hey, Ma," I said, "why do I get the feeling I'm being prepared for a big announcement?"

Jamie and Lewis smiled at each other, and Lewis opened his briefcase and pulled out a sheaf of documents.

"He doesn't miss much these days, does he?" Lewis laughed. "You're bit of a changed character, Ben, since that first night at the hospital."

"Yeah, Lewis, thanks… I think."

"Ben, your case is scheduled for next Wednesday," Lewis said. "There will be a simple summary of the evidence, as you've pleaded guilty to the charges. Judge Beecroft is already working on the sentencing, with all the extra information we've given him."

"Extra information?"

"Yes," Lewis said. "For want of a better description, this is a drug court, where only transgressions that have involved use of drugs are heard. Finally, with crystal meth in particular, the state government is actively pursuing harm minimization policies, rather than spending a fortune on prohibitionist policies. Are you following me?"

I nodded slowly as Jamie cut in. "At last people in my care are now being regarded as patients, not pariahs," he said, firmly. "The government has approved a connection with a new facility in Jomtien Beach near Pattaya in Thailand. I'll be traveling there in two weeks to sign a memorandum of understanding. If the judge is compliant, you may be coming with me as our first patient."

Chapter 23
GUILTY AS CHARGED

JUDGE BEECROFT was an elderly bloke with a shock of white hair, the complete antithesis of who I expected to head up a progressive, cutting-edge court system. Once the formalities were over and we resumed our seats, his intellect was obvious—warm, encouraging, but as sharp as a tack. The police prosecutor read the charges again for the record, and I repeated my plea of guilty under mitigating circumstances.

"And what were those circumstances again, Mr. O'Connor?" he said. "Remind me."

I looked over at Lewis, who winked surreptitiously because I knew Judge Beecroft had already apprised himself of every facet of my case but wanted me to tell my own story in my own words. I repeated everything, word for word, quite wearily but willingly so he could understand I was remorseful.

"The worst day of your life, Mr. O'Connor?" he asked.

"No, Your Honor," I said, "the worst day of my life was at a club several months prior where I tried crystal methamphetamine for the first time. If only I hadn't done that, I wouldn't be standing here now."

"So even if the events that precipitated this action of yours had still occurred and you weren't influenced by your drug-taking, how do you think you may have reacted?"

Lewis looked worried. This was certainly not in the script, but I felt resolute. "Your Honor, I would have simply walked away and helped the admin and sales team who went on to open a new business. That has actually happened, and almost all of Smithson's old customers have deserted him as a result. That would have been infinitely more satisfying."

Lewis was then asked to lay out our defense, calling Jamie as a witness. Judge Beecroft had to be seen to be impartial, and he put Jamie through the hoops. "Professor," he said finally, "what is your recommendation exactly in this case?"

"Your Honor," he said, "we need to assess the effectiveness of the treatment being offered in Thailand. Frankly, it's costing a fortune to dry people out here in Victoria, only to suffer a disappointing degree of recidivism because we don't have the facilities and the funds to finish the job properly. If this 'life therapy' is successful, we'll ask the federal government to underwrite it through Medicare. Mr. O'Connor is the ideal patient, Your Honor. We feel his chances of success are buoyed by his positive attitude."

"Very well. Please stand, Mr. O'Connor."

Fuck, here it comes.

"Benjamin John O'Connor, your actions, albeit under the influence of drugs, could have resulted in the deaths of three people, including your own. No provocation is worth placing the lives of other human beings at risk, whether you used a motor vehicle or some other weapon."

The police prosecutor straightened his shoulders and smiled. It looked like a custodial sentence was going to be applied after all.

"I therefore sentence you to three hundred hours of community service, with no conviction recorded, because there needs to be no complication with passports and immigration in both Australia and Thailand. Professor Weiss, to ensure justice is served, you are to remain responsible for the whereabouts of Mr. O'Connor at all times. On his return to Australia, his community service will comprise working at Waratah Centre, reporting to you, helping other patients overcome their addiction. That is all."

"All rise," yelled the clerk, and we all stood. The police were not happy.

"But an appeal would go nowhere," a jubilant Lewis said.

The big man in all of this, however, was tired. Jamie Weiss looked twice his age, and I decided I would never let him down. I went over and hugged him. I didn't need to say anything, but I gave him the message as best I could.

"Thanks for giving me my life back. It's up to me now," I said.

"Bullshit." He grinned. "It's a team effort. Think of it this way—if you fuck up, all those behind you in the queue don't get a chance, so don't do it for me, do it for them as well."

Chapter 24
RESORT JOMTIEN

I KNEW enough about this place to know that it was different to all the others in Thailand.

To begin with, the location was strange. Jomtien was originally a little fishing village around the corner from Pattaya, which over the years had grown into one of the world's most infamous sex capitals; pretty ugly, full-on stuff. But as Jamie and I were driven through twin white pillars into the garden setting beyond, we might have been in a different world. It felt peaceful, the cacophony of noise from the roads and local markets fading away, like an oasis in a war zone. Reception was in a very laid-back small hotel. I was shown to my room while Jamie was led away to talk to some people, presumably the principals of the business. I showered, changed into shorts and a tee, and lay back on the bed. I knew I was far from being where I should have been. The ten days or so I was allowed to spend with my family had seemed joyous for them, but if I was honest with myself, it was underwhelming for me. Even spending time alone with Peter had been almost a chore, because it didn't press my buttons. In the old days before Tina, I was like a kid myself with him. Walks along the coast over the rocks were exciting back then, mundane in my new world. I found myself gushing over stuff, trying to compensate, and Peter picked it up straightaway.

"You're not well yet, Dad, are you?" he said, and I nodded. I wasn't bloody well yet, but I had to keep trying. I sighed to myself. Here I was in this place, and I wondered how the hell these people could make any difference.

I didn't really expect many similarities with the Waratah Centre, and there weren't. This wasn't a secured facility; patients could come and go as they pleased. Although in my case, Jamie was still responsible for me, and there was no way I'd abuse that privilege. Interestingly, the package included a return to Jomtien twelve months after my "treatment" had been completed. They were determined to track my progress. I felt more like a guinea pig than ever, but it did underscore how serious the project was in terms of returning people like myself to a productive status rather than relying on the social security system to support me. It sounded cold, but those were the facts of life, and I had to suck it up.

ROSS FERRIS was an Australian guy, early thirties, and the liaison between patients, their families, and in my case, my protector in the form of Jamie Weiss. He informed me he would also be working with me directly as a therapist. He'd been an addict himself and now dealt daily with the joy of helping other people. *Fuck*, I thought at first, *this guy's too perfect. He'll start quoting scripture at me soon.* But he didn't. Jamie left to return home two days later, and Ross took me under his wing. He was a gay man, happily settled with a local Thai bloke, and he genuinely loved his job.

"We take care never to discriminate," he said. "It happens we have a preponderance of gay men here at the moment, but every new patient is made aware that this place is very much a mixed bag of sexuality and gender. We have males, females, and trans people here—gay, straight, bisexual, and grateful." He said this with a perfectly straight face.

I stared at him, thinking I'd misheard, but the bastard was winding me up, and he giggled. I laughed out loud at his outrageous humor, and I felt better that I'd made a great mate here as I struggled with my poor fucking brain. Ross explained that group therapy was part of the healing process, everything from yoga to discussion groups and in between.

"Meditation is a big part of our strategy," he said, "and we open your mind with the help of a nearby monastery." He laughed at the expression on my face as an avowed atheist. "It's all right, Ben; you don't have to become a card-carrying, born-again anything. This is a Buddhist monastery, and they have meditation disciplines that are a big help in getting your brain reconnected with

the real you, not someone else, which is the hall-
mark of crystal meth."

I joined a few of my fellow patients enjoying a
light evening meal in the cool, leafy dining room.
They seemed a bit remote, like an exclusive club
where all of us were fucked-up in one way or another, the only thing we really had in common. I
recognized a television presenter and his missus
from Brisbane—occasionally he'd appear in national ad campaigns promoting everything from
cars to toilet paper. I guessed they were both ice
addicts but didn't ask. The last thing I wanted to
do was to blurt out my story. They mightn't be so
relaxed around a criminal like me, although on
second thought, they'd probably tangled with the
law back home as well. Ice didn't discriminate;
the guy looked ten years older without his stu-
dio makeup, and the drug had done the rest. She
looked older than my mother, yet they could only
be in their late thirties.

The remainder of the population appeared to
be single guys. I guessed all of them were gay because they'd taken care to present themselves so
nicely. There was the occasional bit of bling, the
preppy haircuts, and ample evidence of cosmetic
surgery. These days I ate enough to feel full, but
I didn't enjoy my tucker as I once did. The link
between incoming stimulation of any sort and out-
going pleasure was broken, and I felt depressed as
a result.

"Enjoying your meal?" asked Ross, and I
told him truthfully it was a nonevent for me these
days. He nodded and beckoned to a Thai bloke

who appeared in the doorway. He was a little younger than Ross, a handsome fellow with the ageless look most Thai people seem to take for granted. He bent down, and Ross kissed him on the cheek.

"This is Yod, my partner," Ross said. "He runs a travel agency in Jomtien." I stood up and held out my hand, but he beat me to it and gave me the *wai* with his palms together, bowing deeply so his nose and fingers met—a formal and respectful greeting in Thailand, as I later found out.

"Ross will make you better, but you must do what he say," Yod said with a grin. "He get very cross if you don't do what he say. I know."

I laughed for the second time since arriving, which was amazing for me and a tribute to Ross and now Yod. Their humor was bloody contagious, and I began to relax.

Chapter 25
IN THE MIDDLE OF THE NIGHT

THERE WAS little supervision in the evenings. Most rooms opened onto the huge common room where group discussions and yoga took place. There was a type of hip-high planter box running continuously between our doors and the big room, so it seemed quite private. As I'd done at Waratah, I left my door ajar. I didn't like feeling hemmed in; it made me ever so slightly claustrophobic, another little reminder of the nastiness of Tina.

That night I jolted awake and rolled over in bed. My bladder was okay, but something else had woken me. I lay there listening and… there it was again. Someone was crying next door. It was a sound of pure misery, of hopelessness and sorrow. No poor bastard should ever have to feel like that, I thought, and I rolled out of bed and padded out of my room toward the source. I pushed open my neighbor's door and froze in the doorway. What if I intruded on an indignant female—I could get done for attempted rape, for Christ's sake. But the tenor of the voice I heard was very male indeed. As I crept in, I could make him out in bed, a good-looking bloke, well-built and about my age, clearly having a nightmare, poor bastard.

"Hey, mate," I said. "Mate, wake up. You're having bad dreams."

"Huh?" he said, his eyes opening. "Who are you?"

"Your neighbor next door. I'm Ben."

"I'm Matt. Did I wake you? Sorry."

"No worries, mate. You sounded so sad. I couldn't lie there and let you suffer like that."

"Oh, thanks, Ben. Unfortunately it's ongoing, always the same. I can't ever seem to stop, and the drugs made it worse."

"Would you like a cup of tea, Matt? I know where the kettle is."

"You don't have to do that."

"Don't be a silly bitch. I wouldn't offer if I didn't want to. You've fucked up my night anyway, so I'll see if a cuppa works."

His eyes sparkled in the dark as I went into the common room and made two cups. When I returned, he'd switched on the bedside lamp and was sitting with his legs swung over the covers.

"Here you are, mate," I said. "Don't burn yourself—it's bloody hot."

He looked at me with grateful eyes. "Thanks, Ben, you're very thoughtful. No one has ever bothered like that before."

"Well, I have to get a decent night's sleep somehow," I said gruffly, grinning at him to take out the sting.

He sighed. "Sadly, I can't guarantee I won't interrupt you again, Ben. Would you like me to move?"

"No, of course not. We have to help each other here, but can I ask what it's about? You seemed to be repeating 'John, John,' over and over."

Matt lowered his head, and I immediately felt I'd intruded too much into his private world and kicked myself internally. But he reached out, took hold of one of my hands, and stared into my eyes.

"John was my husband. We were an item for five years, married for two years. A drunk driver knocked him down and killed him instantly, and my life changed forever. Drugs of every type and in enough volume to kill an elephant, and nonstop chemsex. That's why I'm here."

Here I was, in the early hours of the morning and on the other side of the world, having found someone with circumstances worse than mine. Not unusual in itself, but I was surprised to feel an overwhelming concern for him. He seemed so vulnerable and yet so nice, and I knew what I had to do.

"You need someone to remind you that you're still a great bloke. How about a bed partner with no strings attached to help you sleep better? It may help me too."

His face lit up; we'd each made a new friend, and he welcomed the offer with a dazzling smile, squeezing my hand.

"Ben, you're amazing, thanks."

We climbed under the covers, and I threw my arm over him, and it worked—we must have gone back to sleep in seconds. The next thing I knew, Ross was calling from the door.

"Wake up, sleepyheads," he said. "Breakfast in ten minutes."

Matt and I looked at each other and laughed. We weren't rooting or doing anything terrible, but we'd shared a bed for part of the night, and our supervisor seemed neither judgmental nor even surprised. If anything, he sounded pleased.

We were both new to Jomtien on the same day, so it made sense to stick together, and it was nice to have a friend who was traveling the same road as I was. We arrived at breakfast, and Ross walked us around the room first, introducing us, putting names to the faces I'd seen last night. Matt was from Sydney, I was from regional Victoria, and that was the end of the detail.

"Food first," Ross said, handing us each a plate and pointing to a nice buffet.

"I really don't eat much breakfast," Matt said.

I stood there and looked at him in disgust. "Listen, you silly bitch," I said. "Don't let the drugs take charge, it's your body, and you need to start looking after it. Breakfast is the most important meal of the day."

"But I've never eaten much breakfast," he repeated.

"Don't fucking whine at me. You have to eat properly. I've lost much of my appetite as well, thanks to Tina, so let's show the drug dealers that we're in charge of our bodies now and we intend to do this lovely food justice, even if we have to cram it in until we're nearly sick."

Ross, I noticed, couldn't stop smiling, perhaps because my little words of encouragement were heard all over the room. I loaded Matt's plate up, then mine, and as we walked to our table, several of the other patients went back for seconds.

"Tea or coffee?" Ross asked, taking our orders and bringing our cuppas to the table. He leaned over and lowered his voice so only we could hear. "Thanks, guys. You did so well. That's exactly what they needed to hear. Now enjoy."

Yoga was next up, but the farting and the lack of flexibility after our gigantic breakfast made it impossible. Our instructor, a diminutive little Thai lady, suggested we go for a nice long walk instead. After a tour around the grounds, she took us down to the beachfront, where we breathed in fresh air from the Gulf of Thailand.

Chapter 26
MEDITATION AND THE MIND

"WE BELIEVE you two will benefit from working together," Ross said, and his cohort, a middle-aged Thai lady, nodded sagely as Ross continued, "While everyone's journey to neural re-education is an individual one, the power of two minds working together can never be disputed, can it, Mae."

She smiled at us both with a look that could only be described as loving. "It is Thai way. If no family, then make new family. Then much better. Nobody alone in Thailand, family look after."

Her reasoning seemed to affect Matt and me in the same way. "Yes, together," we said in unison, nodding away like two little rag dolls.

THE DAYS found some routine, and while the grumbling was vocal at times, everyone seemed to pitch in and cooperate because, I suspected, we all wanted to get better. Trying desperately to find some of the happiness that ice had taken from us was the horrible common denominator.

Yoga was now before breakfast, and we were both amazed to find it wasn't a physical discipline but a soothing and calming influence mentally. After breakfast on the third day, Mae came around smiling with a cane basket.

"People," said Ross, "Mae is collecting mobile phones. We need your full attention, and being in contact with external influences will only slow your progress. I know some of you are trying to do business while you're here. Forget it. Forget social media, forget everything except your fellow patients and the support staff who are working hard to restore your dignity and your happiness. Mobile telephones are a modern invention that are counterproductive to your full recovery at this time."

Matt winked at me as we watched the reaction of the younger gay boys; their looks of horror and confusion said it all.

ROSS BECKONED us over after lunch. "How do you think you're doing, guys?" he asked.

"I feel calmer," Matt said. "Perhaps a bit more hopeful, even."

"The same," I said, "although I still feel depressed because my mind isn't my own yet. Part of it still seems to be with Tina."

Ross nodded. "Don't be too hard on yourself, Ben. I think the reason Matt feels a bit chipper is that you've driven him along at your own expense."

Matt grinned. "I'd agree with that. My turn to take charge for a while."

It occurred to me I'd been leading the pack at home and at work for years, and suddenly someone outside my family had decided to take responsibility for me. I liked the sound of that.

"I want you guys to go over to the monastery first," Ross said, "and live in there for at least two days. You two have such positive energy that the more 'precious' members of the group will try to be more enthusiastic about the experience. It's called teaching by example."

"So what's the objective?" Matt asked, and I thought, *Jesus, this bloke's switched on*.

"The objective is to quieten your minds," Ross said, "remove all the junk, and move toward taking charge of your conscious and unconscious minds, where you can unblock the pathways of the brain and use meditation on a regular basis for the remainder of your days. We leave the teaching process to the monks; you'll be in their care and live under their rules. I promise you it's an experience you'll not forget."

WE WERE met by a monk at the temple gate who was "our man," we were told. He spoke English fluently and filled the role of interpreter as well as supervisor.

"My name is Sun," he said, "and you are Benjamin and Matthew." A smiling, smallish fellow in saffron robes and a buzz cut, he was about our age, and he gave us a respectful wai, which we returned, having been reminded by Ross that showing Thai people we respected their culture was both essentially good manners and also helped us assimilate as guests in their country.

He led us into a hall where we met the abbot, who was seated on an ancient-looking chair on an ornate platform at the end of the room. We bowed our heads in a wai, offering him small bunches of tropical flowers as a token of respect. Immediately his piercing eyes were fixed on us, not judgmentally or crossly, but more analytically. He spoke slowly to Sun, who nodded at us, sweeping his hand over our heads, answering the senior monk's question.

"He says that meditation is an individual's inner quest for peace and well-being. He can't understand why two of you are here at the same time."

We nodded, a bit disappointed that one of us might have to return to the resort, but Sun turned to his boss, and I heard Ross's name mentioned several times. The abbot looked skeptical, then thoughtful, and finally, beaming, he spoke to Sun, nodding.

"Master has only seen this phenomenon very rarely," Sun explained, "where two people share so much of the one mind. Ross is very intuitive and feels your journey could be enhanced if you meditate together, so we will do as he asks."

We were shown our "space," which could never be construed as a bedroom. It had a lumpy mattress of sorts on the floor, and behind a screen in the corner was a hole—with a dish of water beside it.

"Toilet," Sun said. "Your responsibility to keep clean and replace water."

We nodded together; we somehow understood we were on the same wavelength even after a few short days, and so none of this was a real surprise. We certainly didn't expect a five-star hotel, but this would be an experience at the other end—not a hotel, not a school, not a jail, but somewhere in between. The place stunk of bat shit and was made of stone. Steps were worn into hollows from the footprints of devotees. It was a harsh environment, brightened only by prayer mats and some other colorful bling.

Sun then led us to a far corner of the temple, where he sat us in the lotus position, facing each other. "This is phutto," Sun said. "Mindfulness of breathing. You focus on breathing, counting the breaths. After you breathe out, you count one, then you breathe in and out and count two, and so on up to ten, and then you start again at one."

Jesus, this'll be riveting, I thought, and Matt squeezed my hands—busted!

"Stop it," he said. "Concentrate. That's what this is about. Focus on our breathing and let the other thoughts in our poor addled heads slip away, particularly the bad ones."

He squeezed my hands again to say I was forgiven, and we started counting out loud, then to ourselves. We were totally in sync, and we seemed to lose track of time. I began to be aware of all the bad thoughts in my mind, which would present themselves and then slip away: my father scream-ing, Mia and Timmy crying, Andrew Smithson sneering with Grant Hopkins looking innocently over his shoulder.

"Breathe," said Sun. Another squeeze from Matt and I fell back into my mantra. Then I felt other things. Shadows of shouting people, includ-ing a big woman, swearing and pointing, a car wreck, and I realized my connection with Matt had caused me to take on his bad thoughts and bad memories, so I squeezed his hands to let him know we were in this together, and those thoughts slipped away as well.

That night, exhausted, we were pointed to-ward the main hall, where we joined the monks for the evening chant and then prayer, none of which meant much to either of us. But we were pleased to be included as part of our new discipline. There was almost no food—some scraps of bread with bottled water Ross had insisted we drink—and at daybreak we were at it again. We felt faint through lack of food and fitful sleep, but the mists in our minds seemed to clear as we concentrated with-out distractions, earning Sun's praise. All day we honed our new abilities, and toward evening we felt like we were levitating, floating within the quietness of our minds, the peacefulness under our control and linked together.

THE FOLLOWING morning, we were introduced to the next stage, called vipassana.

"This is a return to using your mind, but you do so more selectively," Sun said. "You have a new strength now, an awareness where you observe new thoughts and thought processes. The thoughts that make you happy are yours to keep, but keep the bad thoughts away with phutto every day and the good thoughts will stay with you."

"So every day we should practice meditation, phutto first," Matt said.

"Of course, even while you do yoga. Then with vipassana you must seek good thoughts and good things."

We hailed a tuk-tuk—a pickup truck with unpadded seats under a metal canopy, which found every pothole bouncing back home—and fifteen minutes later, Ross waved as we walked in. He'd obviously spoken to Sun or the abbot because he was all smiles.

"Well done," he said. "You'll probably get questions from your fellow patients. Tell it like it is."

WE GOT back to our rooms, where a shower had never felt better, and found two bowls of steaming tom kha gai with some boiled rice waiting for us, set up on a little table in Matt's room. We ate our food, but I could see Matt struggling a bit with our experiences, and I asked him why.

"That's probably the weirdest thing that's ever happened to me," he said, quite seriously.

"What do you mean?"

"Everyone else except us seemed to think from day one that we were, you know, so close, and I thought, *in your dreams*, and yet here we are a few days down the track and we're virtually channeling each other's thoughts."

"I'm also blown away," I said, "but I don't want to question anything. I've read a lot about the Thai people. They don't have the hang-ups of Western society because they've never been colonized, and consequently the missionaries never got a foothold here. I think I'm beginning to see the big picture. This is an ancient society, a chance for people like ourselves who've fucked up to return to a humbler way of life and hook into the basics, the things that matter."

"You've got a way with words," he said quietly. "What did you do for a living?"

"I was a real-estate agent, but I've also read everything I could lay my hands on because I missed going on to university."

"Real estate, huh? That explains it. You'll probably try to sign me up."

"Would that be so bad?"

"Depends what for." He grinned, and we laughed at each other. We were winding each other up and enjoying it, that's for sure.

Chapter 27
TELL ME YOUR STORY

"MATT," I said, putting it as simply as I could, "crystal meth, as you well know, makes you feel so amazing, like you are the most intelligent, attractive, and popular person on earth. When you stop using and Tina leaves you, everything seems uninteresting, mundane, even boring. There's no excitement anymore, and I have to admit I've thought about dabbling again, except in my case, I'd be back to where I started with one toke, and that's the truth."

"Is that all that stopped you?"

I thought about it. "No, I must have some pride," I said, "some sense of decency remaining. My mother called in two old school friends of hers, one a barrister, the other the guy in charge of government rehab in Victoria, Jamie Weiss. I owe these guys, but my real motivation is Mum. I couldn't do it to her again. She's sold her house to finance my recovery. That was the only thing she had after Dad left."

"When we were meditating, I saw images of a red-faced man screaming and yelling in temper. Was that your dad?"

"Yeah. Like me he had an addiction—except his was booze. We had to call the cops one night when he tried to bash Mum and kill us all. He got jail time for that."

"And I saw two guys sort of sneering at you," Matt said, "laughing their heads off in fact, in business suits."

My heart skipped a beat; the thought of Andrew Smithson and Grant Hopkins plotting behind my back filled me with hatred and bad thoughts all over again. I'd been so busy thinking about good things in the future I'd forgotten about some of the rotten things that had happened in the past.

"Yeah," I said. "That's my ex-boss and his boyfriend, who he appointed sales manager and gave my job." I sighed. "You're talking to a crim. I drove my SUV into the office and woke up in hospital with a copper reading me my rights. I got three hundred hours community service for that little piece of satisfaction."

"That sounds pretty reasonable, actually. They obviously survived, otherwise you wouldn't be here."

"Yes, they did, the cunts, but karma will eventually catch up with them. It's bloody hard for me to forgive them, let alone forget about what they did to me."

"We're probably carrying more shit around than we realized," Matt said thoughtfully. "I've got plenty of my own."

"Let me guess. Your own family, particularly your mother, turned against you," I said.

"Right first time. I'm the second youngest of four boys, brought up in a western Sydney suburb. Mum had our brides picked out for us before we were ten years old. She and Dad weren't only homophobic but aggressively antigay. I hid under the radar for a long time, but my two older brothers outed me when they caught me with a neighbor's kid, and I was kicked out of the family home. My only family contact has been my younger brother, Will. He's a great guy, and we're still in touch."

"So what happened after that? How did you survive?"

"I went on the game and put myself through university, got a business degree, and worked as a client-services manager in an advertising agency. Through the agency I met John, who was developing his own software business. It was love at first sight. We moved in together, five years later he was killed, and you know the rest."

"Jesus," I said, "and I thought I had it tough."

"We all have a cross to bear, but gay boys, even in this enlightened age, still have to be careful when they live in shitheap suburbs like I did. You're straight, Ben. It's always easier for you guys. We still get targeted, and sadly some of us get killed in the process."

The look of disbelief on my face must have given me away. "That's terrible," I said. "Nothing like that happens these days where I live."

"I know it's hard to believe, but it still happens, particularly around the cottages. They're more dangerous than ever." Matt must have seen the look on my face. I blushed, and he frowned. "Don't tell me straight Ben has been doing the cottages in your local town. I don't believe it. You had a girlfriend, didn't you?"

"Yes. Her name was Tammy. She walked out around eighteen months ago. But by mutual agreement, she left her son behind, Peter, and we've raised him, the whole family. He's amazing."

"Ben, don't change the subject. How long have you been doing the cottages?"

"I had a gay mate who gave me head jobs at high school when things were a bit slow and when the chicks were driving me nuts and I was over them. He showed me all the beats around town, how to be cautious and all that good stuff. Gay guys do give better head jobs. I only ever fucked him once, and that was after Tammy left."

"Where is he now?"

"Sill around town and bloody near married."

"Married?"

"Yeah, to my young brother, Tim."

"You're joking!" Matt's face broke into a huge grin, and we laughed. It seemed like a normal thing to do, looked like we were making progress—learning to laugh at ourselves again.

"So, what's chemsex?" I asked after a moment.

"When you use drugs to enhance your sexual experience, often at an orgy held at a dealer's place. I quickly found I couldn't have sex without crystal meth, and that was my downfall. I had an addiction to both sex and drugs, and I'm still fucked-up."

I sat there listening. This poor bastard had been rejected by his family, thrown out of home, worked as a prostitute to feed and educate himself, found someone he really liked, married, then had him taken away. No wonder he had nightmares.

"I reckon we're both improving," I said. "I mean, we've been through the abstinence period in rehab back home. We wouldn't be here if they didn't think we had a chance of a complete recovery."

"I bought my place here," Matt said quietly. "I actually jumped the queue because I was desperate. I had the funds, since we'd sold John's business only two weeks before his death. He'd be livid if he knew our money was being used to get my mind and body back to where it should be. We were going to start a family."

He sniffed, and I flew to comfort him. "It must mean something that we can bloody near read each other's mind," I said, and he gave me a sickly grin. "I've never really had many friends in my life. I've been too busy trying to earn a living, and yet I feel I've met my best friend in a few days."

"Me too."

"So, are you going to sit on your arse and cry the blues all day, or are you going to get on with it, bitch?"

Chapter 28
STEPS ALONG THE WAY

WHILE WE all joined in the group sessions in the mornings, most of our fellow patients were split off for one-on-one treatment and counseling, leaving Matt and me almost to our own devices.

"Frankly, I'm happy as long as you guys spend time with each other," Ross said, "because the longer you're with us, the more obvious is the effect you two have on each other." He must have noticed the skeptical look on my face. "Your friendship is a healing influence," he continued. "If you think for a moment I'm exaggerating, then think again, because I've seen dozens of people in your situation, and none of them are as far advanced as you guys are after only a few weeks." Ross gestured toward one wall of the common room with a wry smile on his face. "Guys, come over here and look at yourselves in the big mirror."

We looked at each other, wondering what he was on about. We stood side by side, staring at our reflection.

"What do you notice about yourselves?" Ross asked.

"We're in quite good shape," Matt said. "The exercise has done us good."

"True, but there's something else. What do you notice, Ben?"

"Well, I suppose we have smiles on our faces most of the time now, rather than being glum pricks."

Matt sniggered, and Ross smiled. "Well, that's true also, but there's something else that is a testament to your friendship, your closeness as two people. Mae noticed it some time ago, and today is no exception. Matt, what color is your shirt?"

"Umm, navy blue."

"And your shorts?"

"Gray."

And Ben, your shirt?"

"Navy blue, and shit, I've got gray shorts too."

"Exactly. Out of the last twenty days, you've worn almost the same color combinations for seventeen days. So now will you believe me when I say your friendship is so close, it's helping you heal? Two very similar minds focused on getting better together."

We laughed at ourselves, but Ross had a point; it actually spooked us a bit that we would unconsciously dress in the same clothes most days, but anything that helped us in our recovery was welcome. We did feel different in comparison to our early days at Resort Jomtien. Rather than better, we both still had some smallish cravings triggered by some simple event, even a remark made by someone unintentionally, so we knew we still had a way to go. What did feel good, however, was Ross's confidence in us, and we caught each other smiling at his praise.

"There's Muay Thai if you feel up to it," Ross said, speaking of the martial art that is a national sport in Thailand. "Por, our maintenance fellow, is actually a Muay Thai Kru—a Master— and the boys, Kit and Aran, are also trainers. I know they're available right now if you'd like some instruction. It's something else you can take away from here and use in your daily lives if it interests you."

Matt seemed so enthusiastic I didn't have the heart to say no, so I nodded like a puppet, and we found ourselves on the grass at the rear of the building, shaded by a huge tree. To my surprise it wasn't what I'd imagined it to be.

Por bowed and drew his hands together in a wai. "Muay Thai is a way of removing anger, stress, and anxiety, improving self-esteem and discipline with new skills."

We were paired with Kit and Aran, with Por speaking quietly all the time. Learning how to kick was a joke; I'd never thought of kicking anyone or anything, in self-defense or otherwise, and I was like a big girl, falling arse over head several times until Matt stopped us and made sure I was okay with the skill before we moved on. We were absolutely buggered after an hour or so, and Por called a halt.

"If we make this part of every day," Matt said, "then at least we'll get ourselves really fit. What do you think, Benny boy?"

I could only grin back at him as I limped away, my muscles aching, but he was right. It was good therapy, sending our minds in a very different direction.

OUR DAYS took on a pattern: meditation in whichever room we slept in, then yoga with the group, then breakfast, followed by Muay Thai, which usually took us up to 11:00 a.m. or so. A few days into Muay Thai, we both felt more than a little sore, and Por noticed.

"Spa," he said, pointing to the tub at the end of the awning, protected by a screen. It was so soothing and beautiful, we nearly slipped off to sleep.

"Out now," said Por. "Massage." Kit and Arun pointed to massage tables set up side by side near the tub as Ross arrived.

"Ah." He smiled. "You're about to experience the part of Thai culture for which the kingdom is most famous—and infamous also!" He glanced at me; the expression on my face must have said it all, and Matt laughed.

"Don't tell me big bad straight Benny is frightened of wandering hands," he said.

"I wouldn't mind if they were yours," I said and left it at that.

Chapter 29
LUNCH

A FEW days later, Ross again cornered us after breakfast.

"Got a moment?" he asked, leading us to a quiet table. "Yod has asked if you would like to go to lunch today in Jomtien. He's got a special treat lined up for you."

"That's lovely," Matt said, "but we're being spoilt by you guys. Is there a special occasion?"

"No special occasion, except both Yod and I were once in the same situation as you two, and we remember the things that helped get our minds back to where they should have been. We're grateful for what we have now, and we try to put back into society what we took out, if you know what I mean."

I nodded. Both Matt and I had talked about considering careers in helping other addicts like ourselves in the future. These blokes were awesome and had faith in us—another reason not to slip back.

Yod had a gentle but firm presence about him; his reputation among the locals was legendary because he was a successful businessman and had a farang as a partner. Farangs were foreigners in Thailand; we knew that, and we were beginning to understand why Pattaya in particular attracted so many Thai boys, men, ladies, and ladyboys from all over Thailand. Farangs were the lifeblood of the local economy, certainly in Pattaya, but not so much in Jomtien.

"Here is where the couples come," Yod said, waving his hand over the main street and down toward Dongtan Beach. "Much quieter here—night life all in Pattaya. Boyztown go all night. I worked there once, before Ross rescue me, then we rescue each other from addiction."

"How long did it take you guys to get your heads right?" Matt asked, and I grinned. Matt didn't waste time beating around the bush; he always got straight to the point.

Yod smiled at us. "About two years from a very nasty beginning until we knew we would never go back to our old drug-fueled lifestyle."

"How did you reach that conclusion?" I asked.

"Ross admit he in love with me, and when he ask me how I feel, I cry."

Matt and I looked at each other in alarm. Our curiosity had got the better of us; we felt ashamed that we'd probably upset Yod with our prying, yet he was looking at us with moist eyes and still able to speak.

A grin lit up his handsome face, and he said softly, "I say to Ross, I love you too. I love you

from first day we meet, but I am too shy to say before. Both of us feel nothing can stop us then. Ross
get job at Resort Jomtien, and my family help me
with my business. I start very small, but we are
now largest in Jomtien."

Seldom had anything moved me as much as
this story. I could imagine what primitive facilities
for drying out were a few short years ago. Matt,
too, was on the same wavelength. No wonder
Ross understood all the patients under his care so
well. Matt and I were lost in our thoughts when
Yod waved his hand toward the main street.

"Come," he said, "we have lunch now, our
treat." He pointed at a nearby building. "Look.
Something from Australia, in case you were
homesick."

The smart, spotlessly clean, modern-looking
premises stood out from the rather mundane hairdressing salons, massage shops, and restaurants
that surrounded it, their spaghetti wiring outside
adding to the chaos. Yod held the door open. It
was an Australian pie shop—everything fresh and
baked on the spot—owned by an Australian guy
with a Thai wife, he told us. It smelled divine. The
pies and the coffee gave off a distinctive aroma
I'd forgotten for so long. The staff were all in uniform, and rather than order a pie and smother it
with tomato sauce, we had a proper menu with sal-
ads, chips, even gravy if you wanted it. We plowed
in as Yod watched, amusement written all over his
face.

"Aren't you eating?" Matt said.

"Yes, I will eat. I love my seafood pie. It is coming now."

Yod's conversation was mostly lost on both Matt and me. I think it was a mixture of home-sickness and delicious food; we weren't about to let anything get in the way of either.

"The pastry's different to home," I said to Matt, who nodded with a full mouth.

"Yes," he answered, "it's like short-crust pastry, but with something else added in."

We had two coffees each to Yod's one, patted our tummies, and sat back in our chairs, smiling like two satisfied felines after a giant saucer of milk.

"Thank you so much," we said in unison to Yod, who gave us a wai and a little bow.

"I must return to work," he said. "I have a large group of Chinese arriving, and everything must be perfect."

We struggled home, deciding to walk because we were so full. At some stage I took Matt's hand and helped him along. It all seemed so natural in Jomtien; two blokes walking hand in hand was not only acceptable but expected if they liked each other, and I liked Matt. He'd turned into my best friend. It'd been explained to me in the counseling I'd had back home that my lack of friendships in my teenage years and beyond was closely linked to an absence of trust brought on by my relationship with my father. Plus, I'd left school early, working any job to help support our family after Dad left. There was no time to make friends or have a social life. That changed, of course, when I started in real estate, but my best friend from there wasn't even a bloke—it was Gloria. She'd been mortified when I'd gotten myself into trouble, and she'd been in touch several times a week during my rehab. But now I had this bloke in my life, Matthew Wilson, and the longer our association went, the closer we appeared to be, to the point where at times during meditation we could practically read each other's minds!

We walked into my room and collapsed on the bed together, then woke up about 4:00 p.m. and made ourselves a cup of tea. We found the boys, Kit and Aran, and had some sparring and kicking practice for half an hour, which seemed to help us digest our magnificent lunch. The evening meal was light, but we enjoyed the soups and rice. It was a perfect day.

WE WERE up early the next morning, did our meditation, then had half an hour of peaceful yoga with our lovely lady instructor. We ran into the breakfast room, claimed our table, and attacked the buffet, loading up our plates. Fruit and muesli first, a cup of coffee, then toast on the side with eggs, bacon, and grilled tomatoes. I went back for some nice-looking feta cheese, and Matt made himself a mini bacon sandwich. We were on our second coffees when Ross came over, a big smile on his face, and gave us each a kiss on the cheek, which I reckoned was lovely. He certainly didn't hold back if he liked you.

"How are my star pupils?" he asked, smiling. "I see you won't starve easily—your appetites seem to have improved. Did you enjoy lunch yesterday?"

"Yes, it was great and very thoughtful of Yod."

"And we had a beautiful dinner last night and a fantastic breakfast this morning," Matt said.

Ross laughed at us while we looked at each other, wondering what the big joke was.

"Remember how you simply ate to stay alive?" We nodded like silly puppets again, but slowly the facts began to register. "Yes," Ross said, "since lunch yesterday, your brain has made a reconnection with your stomach. Think about it. You now enjoy eating again—another victory along the way. Congratulations!"

Chapter 30
DECISIONS, DECISIONS

"DO YOU believe all this mumbo-jumbo that's happened to us?" Matt asked.

"Does it really matter? Ross reckons we're miles ahead of everyone else. As long as we're recovering, who gives a shit how we do it?" I said with a grin, hoping he'd fall in behind me. Matt looked less than convinced, but he had to agree about one salient fact: by any measure, we had sailed past our fellow patients in our program. Almost everyone else had issues of some sort, while Matt and I seemed to be in a calm place, enjoying life like we were on holiday rather than desperately trying to school our brains into working as they should. We knew that had already happened to us. We were enjoying our food, relishing in the exercise of Muay Thai, and had added several laps of the pool to our daily activities. The sole negative in my mind was the reconnection with sex. In my case my morning erections had returned with a vengeance, while Matt's equipment was quite flat, even during the night when I slipped my hand inside his shorts. I presumed he was still on medication, considering his chemsex addiction, but I thought it might upset him if I mentioned it, so I wisely said nothing.

"I wonder what will happen when we leave here," Matt said, thinking aloud. "Will we fuck up because we don't have each other around?"

"Quite possibly," I lied. I had absolutely no idea, so no blueprint for what had happened to us. All I knew was I'd miss Matt so much it didn't even bear thinking about. I hoped he felt the same way. He'd not previously commented on our future, together or apart, and I wondered why. I decided it was time for brutal honesty, and I grabbed his hand. Jesus, I mean, Matt was a gay man, and I was straight, and I was making all the moves. But I tried to focus on life without him, and the thought drove me on.

"Look," I said, "I really like you, and I know you haven't got much to go home to in Sydney. I wondered if you'd like to come home with me. My family would love you."

A shadow passed over his face, but then he smiled, and I knew I had him. "That's very kind of you, Ben. Are you sure your family won't mind?"

"They'll bloody adore you, particularly Peter."

"That's your son. He's adopted, isn't he?"

"Yes. He was Tammy's child by another bloke. She was carrying him when I took her on. She left with a girlfriend and asked me to take full custody, which I did. He's amazing—very intelligent, very loving. I guarantee you'll love him."

"What about your brother?"

"Oh, Timmy's moved out with Kenny. They live at Kenny's parents' house in a separate unit, but they're around home several times a week to be fed by Mum. My sister, Mia, and her boyfriend, Garry, still live with Mum, Peter, and me. They're great. No trouble and a real backstop to Mum, particularly after I lost my mind."

Matt's sadness seemed to return temporarily. "I've got a house full of memories of my life with John, the very thing that triggered my drug use, so I suppose a holiday somewhere else would be sensible for a while. At least you have your family. I don't have anyone in Sydney except my younger brother, Will, and Michael Parker. Michael was John's accountant and manages the investments for me."

"So is it a deal?" I asked, the words tumbling out of my mouth before I realized I was asking for the order like a real-estate salesman.

"Yes, it's a deal," Matt said softly, "but I insist on paying my way. At least money isn't a problem for me, even though it helped create one."

WE WEREN'T surprised when Ross cornered us the next morning and pointed to his office.

"So I reckon you guys have gone as far as I can take you. Now you have the next stage—reintegration into Australian society."

It was obvious we hadn't thought our situation through; we'd assumed after detox in Australia, then with the regimen here in Jomtien, we'd go back to life the way it was before the shit hit the fan.

"You guys will be in a different place," Ross said. "Your mindset has changed, and your attitudes to many things arc quite different. Some people have trouble adjusting to the way they feel, and some families also have problems coping with this 'new' person."

"Ross, you don't have to feed us a line of bullshit, you know. You're talking to the Benjamin and Matthew Show," Matt said, laughing at our mentor so it was impossible for him to take offense. "Benny has already jumped the gun, Ross. I'm going to live with him and his family for a while, so you can relax. We'll continue to look after each other and carry on with our treatment, at least for a while."

"Oh, thank Christ. I was concerned you'd split and lose contact with each other. You guys are really smart, and what's happened to you two is quite rare, though it did happen to Yod and me too. It's so important you both treat your special friendship with the respect it deserves. So pack your bags, bitches. You're going home tomorrow."

Chapter 31
HOME JAMIE, AND DON'T SPARE THE HORSES

IN MATT'S case, traveling back to Australia was all quite straightforward, but I did feel like a criminal on parole; my passport was flagged on arrival. Jamie Weiss was at Immigration to meet us.

"It's okay, Ben, you're now officially home," he said as my passport was stamped and the system notified I wasn't still at large in Asia.

Ross had certainly done his bit, and Matt was expected, his presence welcomed as we were both hugged by a quite emotional Jamie.

"I had faith in you, Ben, but you've exceeded everyone's expectations. I really must congratulate you—by your example you've made it easier for others to follow."

"I was lucky. I've got a good mate who kept me in line," I said, pointing at Matt.

"Oh, get over yourself, princess," Matt said. "You told me you were too shit-scared to fuck up in case this lovely man kicked your big arse."

"I haven't got a big arse."

"You have. It's a perfect target."

"Christ, who let you off the chain?"

"You did."

Jamie laughed at us, his eyes twinkling. I think he wondered what had happened to me. I was like a zombie going to Jomtien; coming home again I must have sounded like I'd had a personality transplant. I knew I didn't sound like the old me, but no one seemed to notice or to care.

THERE WAS a government car waiting; it was about seventy-five minutes to home, and we settled back in relative comfort. I glanced across at Matt, who seemed preoccupied, and I squeezed his hand.

"This is a new experience, isn't it," I said, "going home to a real family? You haven't had one of those for quite a while, have you?"

His eyes looked sad, but he smiled—another example of us reading each other's minds. I felt his sadness and knew what it was about. "Don't be apprehensive, they *will* love you, but you'll probably never be the same again." He giggled and held my hand, and I thought to myself that we seemed to be heading in the right direction, for now at least.

We slid to a stop outside Casa O'Connor. It was late, around 11:00 p.m., but the lights were on and the front door flew open as my son, seemingly grown up overnight, flew into my arms, then dropped me like a hot cake and embraced a startled Matt. I heard the words "Thank you for saving my dad" as he hugged Matt again.

Then Mum was there—a happy, strong, beautiful lady who made sure I was okay, then pushed Peter out of the way to also hug Matt. And on it went. Mia was blubbering and Garry not much better, and then Kenny and Tim slipped around behind us, Kenny being more Chinese and formal while Timmy was trying to squeeze me to death.

Despite my protestations, Matt had insisted he have his own bed, if not his own room, in a house full of strangers. I explained he could have both—the room across the hall from mine—but I had a sneaking feeling our sleeping arrangements wouldn't change. I was in bed less than ten minutes and he was there, smiling, slipping under the covers with me. We were too tired to talk about it and cuddled up, falling into a deep slumber as we always did. I imagined it would be similar to Jomtien, where we swapped rooms depending on our mood. Yes, it was a strange arrangement, but according to Matt himself, it had become a lovely habit that prevented him from having nightmares, which still haunted him periodically. And in my case, I had to admit I'd never slept better in my life… ever. Occasionally I'd sneak away to relieve the pressure, because my equipment was pretty close to 100 percent functional, and if I was honest with myself, Matt really turned me on big-time.

THE NEXT day I reported officially to Jamie Weiss at the Waratah Centre to begin my three hundred hours of community service. I wilted toward the end of the day. I was taught to do the myriad of cleaning tasks necessary, with an interesting security overlay that involved second-guessing patients who were trying the same tricks as I'd used some months prior.

Matt took Mum's car and drove Peter to school, while Mia and Garry went off to work as usual. After not quite twenty-four hours, it seemed like Matt had always been part of our crazy family. He and Mum seemed thick as thieves, and by 6:30 p.m. a roast leg of lamb appeared, served up with Mum looking shell-shocked. Matt had done it all and told Mum to rest. There was enough for everyone, including Tim and Kenny; they were on the way in as I arrived home in my humble little Toyota. Peter loved his food and was in foodie heaven—he could put away more in one meal than I could eat in a week. He had second helpings, picked at the scraps, and then there were sweets, a bread-and-butter pudding, no less. Mia, Garry, and Mum were all smiles. For someone who should have been suffering from jet lag, Matt was full of energy.

"Now," he said, "Benny tells me you're my new family. Good. I don't know how long I'll be around, but I've appointed myself chief cook. Everyone happy with that?"

I nearly pissed myself as they all nodded their heads like little dolls, including Mum, who normally ran the place with an undemocratic attitude. Now it was Sergeant Major Matt running the place, and Mum looked relieved.

"You're on clean-up duty, Peter, and you're helping, Kenny and Tim. There's tea and coffee to follow." Mia and Garry looked like they'd won the lottery, then spent the proceeds as Matt added, "And you two are rostered for tomorrow night, so won't that be lovely? Mary can have a nice rest."

Chapter 32
DISCOVERY

IT HAD been over seven weeks of penance at Waratah Centre. Some weeks had been well in excess of forty hours—more like fifty, and one bad week even more. But it was good, satisfying work, with much more variation than I'd imagined. I was basically given enough informal training to be a nursing aide, but supervised by qualified staff. Some patients were bloody difficult, but I'd been there myself and knew what their next response would be, so I was able to bullshit them and get the job done. Others were a total physical mess—diarrhea, vomiting—so I was changing bed linen several times a day in some cases. I knew enough not to get involved with patients but developed a lot of friendships with fellow staff members. But above all, I felt good about myself at last, able to feel I'd actually achieved something more in life, putting stuff back instead of taking out.

Matt decided he'd spend a day at work with me after Mum took over her own kitchen for a day. I proudly showed him my duties, explaining the initial process of drying out patients, which wasn't all that different from our own experiences, and then the more mundane tasks of stripping beds, doing laundry, and waiting on tables at lunchtime.

Matt stopped at a door that was closed. "This one in isolation?" he asked, and I nodded. Some of the more problematic people, like I had been, were literally incarcerated under lock and key for a time, and this was such a case. Matt studied the name on the door, then looked at me, turning pale. "Jake Williams. Where does he come from?"

I thought for a moment and then remembered, "Cabramatta, a suburb of Sydney."

"Yes," Matt said in a funny voice. "Are you nearly ready to go home?"

"Umm, yes. I'll clock off," I said, staring at Matt. "Did you know him?"

"I thought I might, but it would be too much of a coincidence. Let's go home and have some family time."

JAMIE WEISS was never far away. In fact we touched base almost every day, and for a man in his position, I found that both endearing and amazing.

"I'm quite fascinated with your return to the human race," he said in response to my question. "I've spoken at length with Ross at Jomtien, and it's extraordinary how you and Matt have worked together to produce a result that demonstrates in both cases that we can rehabilitate people properly and prepare them for a resumption of their productive lives."

"As tax-paying citizens."

"Correct. That's what gets the attention of government. For your information, Ben, there are now a total of seventy-five people from three states who have qualified for Resort Jomtien. We don't expect them all to turn out like you and Matt, but the die is cast, the parameters are set. However, the final legal step for you involves a visit to Judge Beecroft, who needs input from you to assess the success of the program. I imagine he'll ask you about resuming your career. I take it you'll return to real estate?"

"No, definitely not. Even though Gloria Dixon has a place for me, I want to work here."

I'd never seen Jamie Weiss look confused, but there's a first time for everything.

"Here?"

"Yes. I've done some research with Mum's help, and I do my general training starting with next year's intake, then specialize in psychiatric nursing. Hopefully I'll find a position here with you guys. I have all the wrong experience, which helps me understand your patients. You might say that you've inspired me."

The big bloke jumped to his feet, eyes shining like he'd been reborn. "You've given me the greatest reward any medico could ever hope for," he said. "What can I do to help you?"

"Marry my mother."

Chapter 33
GLORIA DIXON REAL ESTATE

GLORIA HAD been in touch almost daily since "the incident," even while I was in Thailand, always encouraging me and never tolerating a bad word about me. Yes, she remained my nearly best friend, second only to Matt and Mum, understanding, with a woman's intuition, why Matt was so important to my complete recovery. She also understood why I'd decided to change careers, even offering to bankroll my nursing studies. And there were two other people whose loyalty was unquestionable—Phillip and Amanda. Matt and I were invited to the sales meeting the Monday morning following the end of my community service time. We supplied the buns, Gloria the coffee.

"This isn't a social visit," I said. "Show me what you're working on."

They all laughed at me, but I was proud of them. The thoroughness of their work was obvious, driven by careful research and a knowledge of each area in terms of resale and presentation, something that Andrew Smithson thought unnecessary.

"Have a look at these," Gloria said. "These are all from last week." She flashed a list of emails and social media messages on the screen. My jaw dropped, and even Matt was impressed. Every single one praised the attitude of sales staff, the information they provided, their courtesy and professionalism.

"Jesus," I said, "a bit different to Smithson."

"Ah yes." Gloria smiled quite evilly. "It's been lovely taking business off dear Andrew and his boyfriend."

"Boyfriend?" said Matt. "This gets more interesting all the time. So the bloke he promoted over you was his boyfriend?"

"Umm, yes. Grant Hopkins."

"Yes," said Gloria, "but there's more. We stand a very good chance of being the only real-estate office in this suburb. I doubt if the principals of Smithson Real Estate will be in any position to open the doors, let alone sell properties."

Bloody Gloria. She not only knew what was going on, I suspected her of social engineering in the background; a seemingly careless comment from her could change the course of world events.

Phillip and Amanda sat transfixed, and Matt looked on, a grin on his face. He'd already worked Gloria out.

"So come on, spill," I said. "You've been saving this up for me, haven't you?"

"No, it only came to a head, as it were, last night, and I had the facts confirmed only half an hour ago."

"And?"

"Well, if you remember, I mentioned our Andy Pandy and the lovely Grant were hosting orgies at the Regal Hotel?" Amanda, Phillip, and I nodded while Matt simply smiled. "Well, you see, those little events were awash with cocaine, and that made them so careless. I mean, many of the attendees—*of both sexes*, I might add—were less than sixteen years of age."

"Jesus, what idiots. It makes my transgressions pale into insignificance."

"Indeed, Benny." Gloria smiled. "I once thought it was such a pity you didn't finish Andy Pandy off with the BMW, but karma has caught up with him and his disgusting little friend anyway, in a much more satisfying manner."

"You're enjoying this, aren't you?" Phillip said. "But tell us what's happened. Don't leave us hanging like this, boss. I can't stand the suspense."

"Remember how he used to go on about the Eleventh Commandment?" Gloria grinned. "Well, someone mentioned to a doting parent that their less-than-perfect child was seen going into Room 454 at the Regal Hotel, so the police were called to open the door without first knocking, and guess what they found? Lines of coke everywhere and young ladies and gentlemen with their legs in the air."

"Gloria, you should write a book," Matt said, holding his sides.

"No money in that," she said. "It's enough to reflect that people should listen to their own advice—if one intends to be naughty, then don't get caught."

Chapter 34
LOVE IS A
MANY-SPLENDORED THING

I DON'T know when it started, but I'm pretty sure it was that first night at Jomtien, when I heard Matt crying. I immediately wanted to protect him. It was like I'd been called to fix part of myself that was hurting, and I'd crawled into his bed, cuddling him up without a second thought. From that point on, we were (and have been) totally inseparable. We actually read each other's minds on occasion—not all the time, but when important decisions have to be made, we're always in sync with each other. We go grocery shopping for the house and agree on every single item. He looks at me and shakes his head like I'm the other half of his brain, and ditto in my case. The point is that the intensity of our relationship, for want of a better name, had increased since I came home from Thailand. With my debt to society paid in full, I now had time to think of myself, and my mind was full of Matt. How he smiled and walked, how he coped with running a home, helping Peter with his lessons, teaching him stuff even though my son was a prodigy. Matt always had space for me, however, and made sure we had some alone time every day.

I cornered Mum one night nearly eight months after my return home, when our lifestyle was lovely, everyone relaxed and cool. Mum, in fact, was the most laid-back I'd seen her since Dad had been removed from our lives. She and Jamie Weiss had a lovely, comfortable relationship where they enjoyed each other's company and shared a mutual love of orchestral music. Like Matt and me, they always found time for each other, despite incredibly busy careers. They still lived separately, but I reckoned that would change in good time.

"Mum," I said, "what does it mean when you think about one person all the time, that you feel really happy when they smile at you and get upset when they're sad, that you miss them when they're not around, and your heart beats like buggery when they give you a kiss?"

"Why, dear, it means you're in love. And thank heavens, because I don't think you've ever experienced that, have you?"

"No. First time I heard people at school talking about chicks with a crush on someone, I thought they were weird. Later on I wondered what all the fuss was about. To be honest, I watched people getting married and thought they were stupid, particularly as so many of them were having a bit on the side."

Mum smiled her beautiful smile, and I noticed she looked years younger since she and Jamie had become an item. "But this is different, dear, isn't it, and you know you want to spend the rest of your life with him, don't you?"

"I've never felt this way about anyone, Mum. I'm fascinated with him. I couldn't bear if something happened to him, but...." Mum looked at me expectantly. Suddenly I knew what was behind her smile. "You never asked me why I jumped the fence, Mum. You acted like you expected it, even after years of my telling you I wasn't gay."

"Therein lies a tale, doesn't it, dear? Things have moved on since your father's ranting and raving. People's sexuality in this modern day and age is much more fluid than they ever thought it was, as you've found."

"The only thing I've found is that I've always been as gay as Christmas. I was in denial until I met Matt."

"Does he understand that?"

"No, I don't think so. Not yet. But I feel... liberated."

Mum laughed again. "Imagine what you father would have said—two gay sons and a daughter pregnant outside marriage. He'd be frothing at the mouth."

"Pregnant? Mia's preggers?"

Mum was beside herself. "Oh, she'll be annoyed I told you. Can you please—"

"I'll pretend I don't know. Sure, for you, anything."

Chapter 35
DAMP EYES

I WALKED into the house quite late. My three hundred hours of community service had long passed, but Jamie had me working my tits off with more admissions than we could comfortably handle. The money was good, however, and I wasn't complaining. It was still a pittance compared to the real-estate industry, but I knew I'd found my career at last, and I was a happy camper.

Mia was sitting in the kitchen, sobbing her heart out, and Matt was holding her hands in his, quietly trying, it appeared, to stem the flow. Garry did what he did best in a situation like that—nothing. And our beautiful Mum looked like the world was on her shoulders.

"So, what's going on?" I asked, having an idea that in pregnant ladies, emotions tended to over-run everything else.

"I'm pregnant!" Mia shouted.

"Oh, little sister, how wonderful," I said, sounding totally surprised even though Mum had already spilled the beans.

"It's not bloody wonderful, Benny. We're up to here with debt," she said, indicating a position somewhere near her neck, "and we can't afford a new house and a new baby at the same time. Sorry."

"Don't talk shit, Mia," Matt said, cuddling my sister, who began blubbering again. "I'll cover the debts so you can start your family. Simple. Now if you'll stop irrigating the floor, we can sit up and eat. Poor bloody Peter has started gnawing at the doorframes."

The sniffling stopped, and despite the upset, my sister ate like a horse—or at least for two people. Every now and then her eyes would swing up from her plate and focus on Matt, who squeezed my hand under the table and gave me a humungous stiffy. It was Mum and Peter's turn to clean up, but Matt beckoned us all into the big lounge room.

"Look, you two," he said to Mia and Garry, "I have the funds to do this for you because my late husband and I sold his business for a large sum of money a few days before he died. I don't ever need to work again, and I have a large discretionary amount at my disposal I've not had the opportunity to put to good use. When John died, all I did was to go crazy with grief, take drugs, and fuck up my life, until I met Benny. He stabilized me and brought me home to where I found the family I always wanted and where I've been at peace at last. And I'll do the same for everyone else in the family so we don't favor one over the other."

For once, my mad mob was quiet, the message sinking in. I could see they all thought it was pie in the sky, and their eyes turned toward me for verification.

"It's true," I said. "I don't know all the figures, but if Matt promises you something, then you will have it. He doesn't tell fibs."

Chapter 36
A STEP ALONG THE WAY

IT SEEMED I was walking along on air, my silly big clodhoppers not even touching the ground. I was being nice to people I hardly knew. Not that I'd been rude or indifferent to them in the past; it was like I had this feeling of bonhomie, and I felt like spreading the joy because I was in love. I literally skipped into work, and Jamie noticed, of course. He probably read me almost as well as Matt. I walked past his office, and he waved me in.

"How's my favorite nursing aide in training?" he asked, a wicked smile on his face.

I looked him straight in the eye. "I'm scintillating, thank you, boss man."

"What does that mean?" he asked, knowing full well what I meant, determined to draw it all out and embarrass me.

"It means I'm very well, physically and mentally, in the finest possible manner and super-deluxe happy about it, thank you so much for asking."

It was clear he wanted to talk because he pointed to the chair alongside his desk. "Benny, I've never seen you like this. You're practically glowing. You're in love, aren't you?"

I smiled and nodded, giving nothing else away.

"It's Matthew, isn't it?"

"Yes. Looking back I reckon it began the first night we met in Jomtien, and it's grown on me ever since. Every day that goes past, I'm a bit more smitten."

"But Benny, you've done a complete U-turn on your sexuality. Was it the treatment we gave you?" he said with a grin, obviously knowing what a silly question he'd asked.

"No, and it was nothing to do with the food either." We laughed at each other, but I wondered to myself why so many straight men, even trained medical professionals, were infused with an insatiable curiosity about gay sex, let alone same-sex relationships. My mother had pointed out that sexuality was very fluid these days, and yes, it was. "Look, can we have a private conversation, Jamie? This is a bit embarrassing for me because I didn't get to where I am in the conventional manner." I may as well have been speaking Swahili for all that Jamie understood what I was talking about; a frown crossed his handsome features, and I couldn't help but think what a ripper stepfather he would be.

"Well, Dad was violently homophobic," I said, "and that's putting it mildly. He drilled into me how gay people should all be executed, that there was never a reason for them to exist, that tolerance of their lifestyle would ruin society. When, as a twelve-year-old, I suggested that gay people were born that way, that it was never a matter of choice, he went ballistic, screaming and shrieking, totally off his head. So even though I really liked gay people, that constant conditioning at home must have had an effect on me. Females came on to me all the time at high school, and the sex was okay, I guess. No complaints except I had the feeling *is that all there is*? It was all underwhelming, but it was a gay mate of mine who introduced me to, ah, blow jobs, gay blow jobs. Sorry, Jamie, I meant oral intercourse."

The big fellow chuckled. "Fellatio if you want to be pedantic, and so far, your story sounds pretty normal for a teenager, except the background at home."

"Yeah, Dad turned me into an arsehole like himself—a hard, uncaring prick who had to turn around and help support our family because he was incapable."

"But you *were* caring, Benny. You worked your arse off to raise your sister and brother."

"And ended up with a chip on my shoulder, hating the world and using people like I'd been used. My gay mate Kenny showed me how the cottages worked, and even when Tammy and I were cohabiting, I'd call in for a blow job. I tried to pretend it was quite normal for straight guys to do this, but the truth is, I enjoyed it a lot more than I cracked on."

I surprised myself with my honesty, but somehow I felt better because of it. "Now you know more about me than anyone, including Mum," I said, "but thanks for listening. It helps."

"My beautiful young man, I'm honored that our trust in each other allows us to unburden ourselves. You're not the only one who has lived on both sides of the fence, as it were, but what made you change and be so sure of your sexuality at this point in your life?"

"As we were saying earlier, I fell head over my silly heels in love, and I knew I'd found my life partner. I know I want to be monogamous, and I also know I want to get married."

"Have you asked him yet?"

"No, that's tonight."

Chapter 37
SHOCK WAVES

I SOMEHOW got through my day. I didn't ring Matt because I knew he was busy with Peter on a school assignment. I did some shopping for fruit and veg and was home early for a change. Our house has its own little car park, a concrete apron where the first vehicle out in the mornings gets parked. That's why I found it strange that Matt's little car was parked in the end of the big garage, because he usually drove Peter to school before Garry, Mia, and I left for work. Mum had her own space, and it was empty because she was on night duty to help out a friend. I walked in, finding the front door locked for a change, and I remembered it was Matt and me for dinner. Mia and Garry were at the movies, and Peter was staying over at a friend's place—hence Matt's car parked out of the way. The light was on in the kitchen, and my spirits rose. *The timing's exactly right for tonight.* I would lay our future out, logically and sensibly, and he would see things my way. I was sure he would.

"You there, darl?" I said, but there was no answer. I walked over to the bench and put down the
shopping I'd done at his request, and there was
still no answer. I walked up to the bedrooms, and
by the time I turned the lights on, it was obvious
no one was home. The mystery deepened. He always let me know where he was, and this was…
disturbing, to say the least. I walked back to the
kitchen, scratching my head, wondering what
to do next, when I saw a large manila envelope
standing between two vases on the dining table;
I'd walked straight past it earlier. *Must be some
mail for me.*

It was for me, but it hadn't come through the
post. It had Ben in block letters on the front. Suddenly my blood ran cold as I tore the thing open.
There was a word-processed sheet and several
bank deposit slips. I recognized my main account,
Mum's, and a little account that we put spare
change in for Peter. I grabbed the letter and began
reading, a feeling of dread sweeping over me as I
guessed what had transpired.

> *Dear Ben,*
> *I'm very sorry I couldn't do this
> another way, but it would be very
> wrong of me to stay any longer with
> you and your family. My feelings for
> you have grown to the point where I
> care for you much more than I should.
> Put simply, I'm a gay man, and you're
> a lovely straight bloke, and an inti-
> mate long-term relationship between*

*us would never work. Hopefully, you
will find a nice girl, settle down, and
have kids. Please apologize to your
lovely family; I hope they understand
why I have to leave and not return. If
it's any consolation, they are the only
family I've really ever had. I was accepted without question from day one,
and I'll miss them terribly, particularly
Peter. I've left funds for everyone as I
promised, deposited in the appropriate
accounts—as you quite correctly said, I
always keep my word.*

*Stay well, Ben, and thank you for
all you've done for me.*

Matt

Panicking, I rang his mobile and got a "this number is no longer in service" message. I tried desperately to remember his home address in Sydney, cursing myself for not being more attentive to detail. I remembered his accountant's name, however—Michael Parker. I searched the online directory and found him, and dialed the number breathlessly, but of course it was after hours, with a bloody recorded message. I sat down on the floor with my head in my hands and cried with frustration and a huge sense of loss, coupled with a feeling of hopelessness. He didn't want me to find him. He'd disappeared into thin air.

Chapter 38
THE HUNT BEGINS

MIA AND Garry were home around 10:00 p.m. By that time I'd calmed down a little, but I still felt like shit. I was blaming myself for fucking up my life yet again, and I knew I was in a bad place, without having the faintest idea how to get him back. The moment Mia walked in the door and saw my face, she knew something was wrong. I showed her the letter. After she read it, she handed it to Garry, who looked like he was about to burst into tears. Through my pain, I realized it wasn't only me that would feel the loss of Matt, but the entire family group.

I spread my hands. "What are we going to do?" I said and lost it totally.

Garry picked me up like a rag doll, carried me to the big comfy sofa, and enveloped me in his typical bear hug, while Mia started cooking eggs.

After I'd eaten, we sat around with a cup of tea. "What am I going to tell Peter?" I said, knowing his reaction would be extreme; the loss to

Peter would be far worse than when Tammy left. He and Matt adored each other.

"You tell your son the truth," Mia said. "He's intelligent, and you'd insult him by telling him fibs. Show him the letter, and he'll work through it himself... with our help, of course."

I slept only fitfully that night, the peaceful sleep of Matt and me cuddled up seemingly gone forever. The next morning I struggled out. I had a rough plan in my head, but I would need a leave of absence from Waratah Centre and Jamie Weiss's blessing before I went anywhere. I showered, dressed, and as stressed as I was, the smell of bacon cooking got my attention. Mum, still in her hospital gear, was cooking me breakfast, and I felt slightly better about life in general.

"Mia told me your news, dear. Stay calm, sit down, and eat," she said, and I did. I helped clear away, showed her the letter, and she nodded, full of wisdom as usual.

"There was always something there, dear," she said. "I couldn't put my finger on it. He was happy, but he had moments of fear sometimes when you two were at your closest. But you have to find him and tell him how you view your own sexuality, a fact of life I've always understood, even if you haven't."

A mother's intuition. How right she was. But this wasn't going to find Matt.

"Ben, I know this is terribly hard on you because it looks like he's rejected you," Mum continued, "but he hasn't. He's terrified of his own feelings for some reason. Maybe he's still grieving

for his late husband, but don't overlook the fact
that he's in love with you. He said so."

"So what are you trying to tell me, Mum?" I
asked.

"That things have a way of resolving themselves, particularly when people love each other
as much as you two do."

I RANG Jamie on the way to work to ask him if I
could see him very early, and minutes later, I sat
down with him. He looked startled as I handed
him the letter, and then nodded as he read it.

"You need to find him quick smart, mate, and
you'll need a leave of absence, won't you?"

Before I had a chance to answer, he started
rattling away at the keyboard on his desktop. I had
compassionate leave on half pay for a month, and
a smiling boss asking me if I needed more cash,
which he'd give me from his own pocket.

"Think about what you need to achieve," he
said. "Don't run all over the place. You need to
plan this, because young Matthew clearly doesn't
want to be found, certainly at the moment. And
take care, Ben. I have a feeling this situation will
resolve itself in the long term anyway."

"That's what Mum said."

Chapter 39
SEARCHING HIGH AND LOW

GLORIA WAS magnificent as always. My new lifestyle was no surprise to her; she claimed she'd understood the partnership the moment I introduced Matt, and that made me feel both better and worse.

"What do you plan to do?" she asked bluntly.

I gazed at her, not sure why I came to her with my troubles, except that she was my best friend and more street smart than anyone I'd ever met.

"Well, he lived in Sydney with his late husband, but I can't remember their address. I certainly can't imagine him going anywhere near his family. They're obviously really feral. They threw him out of home when he was a teenager, his mother even more aggressive than his old man."

"What for?" Gloria demanded.

"Because he was outed as gay by one of his older brothers. The only family member who he even talks to is his younger brother, Will, who's evidently more modern and a bit decent."

"What were his parent's names?"

"Ah, ah, Bernice and William, or Bill."

"So this Will, he's the youngest, right?"

"Yes."

"You have any idea where he lives? Is he married?"

"I think he's married, but I don't have a clue where he lives."

"Okay, so given that his mother sounds like a real bitch, I'll bet the eldest kids have her family names. Maybe the youngest is named after Daddy?"

I shook my head. I had no idea.

"What suburb did his family come from?"

I wracked my brains, and then I remembered something about Cabramatta.

"Let's have a look." She pulled up a list of names, addresses, and phone numbers in that suburb. "Bingo!" she roared. "Here's a W. H. Wilson. Let's give the bastard a call." She switched on the speaker.

"Yeah," came the response.

"Is that Bill Wilson?" Gloria asked.

"Yeah, so what do you want, and who the bloody hell are you?"

"I'm Karen Whitehouse," she lied, "and I'm looking for the next of kin of Matthew Wilson."

"Is he dead?"

"No, not that we're aware of, but he's gone missing."

"Oh, what a fuckin' shame. I thought we might get a slice of his estate."

"So, you *are* his father."

"Well, who the fuck are you? I'm not sayin' any more unless some folding crosses me palm."

"I represent a client who needs to find your son because he is now a beneficiary of a rather large estate."

"How much?"

"I'm not at liberty to say, but there will be a service fee of five thousand dollars payable to the person providing information that successfully leads us to locate Matthew."

"He's a fuckin' poofter. He's no right to any money. He's a waste of space, and we haven't seen him since he left home—and that's about ten years ago."

"What about your younger son, Will. Would he know Matthew's whereabouts?"

"We hardly see him either. He lives at Liverpool."

"Thank you, Mr. Wilson, we'll be in touch."

I couldn't believe my ears. Gloria sounded like she'd been doing this sort of thing all her life. "Won't he be able to trace your call?" I asked.

"Not on this phone." She smiled gleefully, holding it up. "But human greed is evident everywhere, and the silly cunt told us all we want to know."

"But you knew exactly how to find them, then which buttons to push," I said.

"You and I met after I'd begun my career in real estate. I had another one I never talk about except to those close to me, like you." She smiled. "I was formerly Detective Inspector Gloria Dixon. I was retired because of PTSD—I was wounded in a drug raid in the northern suburbs of Melbourne, and my partner was shot dead beside me. My physical injuries healed, but I was facing years of rehab before I got my head on straight again. My therapist advised me to try something totally different, and I worked at several real-estate agencies until I went to Andrew Fuckface Smithson."

"Sorry, Gloria, I didn't know."

"That's because you've never been a nosy, gossipy type interested in other people's business," she said. "You take people at face value, and you are a true friend—you would have been a good mate to me even if I'd been an axe murderer."

We laughed at each other, and it lightened the atmosphere a little, but she caught the desperation in my eyes and decided to press on, searching the Liverpool directory and finding ten Wilsons with an initial of W.

"Most younger people don't bother with a landline these days. We need some horsepower on this," she said, trawling through her own directory until she found what she wanted and placed the call.

"Hello, Simon," she said, the words rolling effortlessly off her tongue. I smiled at her antics; it was clear she'd never lost touch with her previous network, and then another fact hit me. Gloria could be a loyal friend but a mortal enemy when she was defending her friends, and I reckoned I now knew who told the kid's parents about Room 454 at the Regal Hotel.

Chapter 40
A LOT OF NOTHING

THE FOLLOWING morning, I rang Michael Parker, Matt's accountant in Sydney. To say he was unfriendly was an understatement.

"I suppose you're not happy with the money Matthew has given you," he snapped as an opening statement.

"I would give it all back to have Matt home."

"Oh, a bleeding heart. I'm sooo sorry if I offended you. I was his husband's best friend, and I can tell you if Matthew decides to settle down again, it won't be with a lowlife like you, it will be with someone like me, because I have a special relationship with him. If I hear a peep out of you, my friend, I'll call the police. Wouldn't it be interesting if we found evidence of coercion in securing that enormous amount of money from him?"

Mr. Parker cut the connection before I could object. It was probably for the best before I said something I might regret later. However, I recorded every word, as Gloria had instructed.

WITH GLORIA'S connections we found Will, Matt's younger brother. He seemed really nice but had only had one phone call from Matt recently, and that was a few days ago.

"No idea where he was. He said he'd moved on from you guys but not to worry, and importantly, he was sober and intended staying that way. He said he was traveling within Australia, and he'd give me a call if he decided to go overseas."

"Could you call us if you hear from him again, Will?"

"Of course, mate. He talked a lot about you, how you kicked the ice habit together. What happened? Why did he leave?"

"I really don't know. He left a note saying he was getting too deeply involved, and a gay bloke and a straight bloke didn't have any future together. About the same time this was running through his head, I finally realized I wasn't straight anyway."

"Did you tell him that?"

"I didn't have time. He pissed off."

Will gave a sympathetic chuckle. "I think I know what that's about, Ben. He hasn't told you the full story, obviously."

My innards contracted in fear. The unknown might be something I didn't need to know, and while it might hold the key to Matt's behavior, I somehow doubted it would help me to find him any faster.

"When the 'rents kicked Matt out, he moved two streets away in Cabramatta," Will said, "to a mate's place. Jake, Jake Williams."

My mind went into overdrive. Somewhere I'd heard or seen that name, but for the life of me I couldn't remember where.

"Jake was an only child," Will continued. "His parents were quite comfortable, and they welcomed Matt, thank Christ, because otherwise he would've been sleeping rough. They were really good to him and were horrified that Mum and Dad threw him out of home."

"Was he the guy your older brother caught him with?"

"Yes, but Jake was straight, and he wanted to experiment with Matt when silly fuckin' Kevin caught 'em at it. He told Dad, and it was on for young and old, mate."

Will sounded very old-fashioned and lovely, and his loyalty to Matt shone through. I promised myself when all this shit was over and I found Matt, I'd find a way to show my gratitude.

"So he moved in with the Williams family, and after a while Jake decided he liked what he'd sampled. So he and Matt became an item, and they were really, really close, like they were in love, mate."

"So what happened?" I asked.

"Well, after about two years, Jake decides he wants to try some pussy, and he arrives home with this chick. She was actually quite nice, but Matt spat the dummy and moved out overnight. That's when he went on the game, lived upstairs at

this brothel, and put himself through university."
I gasped, but Will giggled. "Mate," he said "the
place was bloody beautiful, and Matt had a little
self-contained unit there, with its own entrance.
He studied like mad but had to take on a certain
number of clients a week. After that his time was
his own."

"Yes," I said. "I think I know the rest of the
story, how he met John, their business, then the
accident followed by the drugs, like me, but what
happened to Jake?"

"Mate, he kept trying to get back with Matt,
over and over, but Matt wouldn't budge. In fact I
called around to Matt's place once when Jake was
there, and Matt told him to get out or he'd call the
cops. You see, mate, Matt is a one-person person,
and Jakey boy thought he could have the cake and
eat it too, the dumbarse shithead. He eventually
fucked himself up big-time on drugs. The last time
I saw him he was flyin' high, didn't even know
who I was."

Finally the penny dropped. Jake Williams had
spent time at the Waratah Centre. Matt noticed
his name on the door to his room, and I found his
Cabramatta address. No wonder Matt had freaked
out. It simply accelerated his departure. No wonder he didn't trust straight guys.

Chapter 41
URGENCY OF ACTION

I WAS comforted by the fact that Matt seemed to be alive and well; we still had no idea where, but we thought he'd be in touch with Will again and hopefully quite soon. Gloria convinced me that running up to Sydney was counterproductive, and that hiring a private investigator wouldn't necessarily get us a result and would cost a fortune. At this stage, therefore, it was life as usual. I returned to work early, my heart bloody broken, but realizing I had to keep going and hope Matt came back. I tried his old phone number every day, but it still had the disconnected message, and I plodded along like I was on autopilot.

"Stay close, Benny," my mad boss shouted as I walked past his office on my second day back. "Come in here, please." Jamie pointed to the nearest chair, then gestured for me to close the door. *Fuck, what have I done now?*

He finished his spirited conversation with a flourish, placing his phone facedown on the desk, and looked over at me. "We have a conundrum," he said quite seriously, staring into space while speaking. "This virus emanating from Wuhan in China may have truly destructive potential, like kill thousands of people. Already quite a few Chinese people have lost their lives."

We'd all been watching morning television, whose sole content seemed to be talking about what appeared to be an epidemic, and we wondered what effect it would have on us.

"How serious is it, Jamie?"

"To be honest, I don't know at this stage, but the feeling in the medical community is that it will get much worse, even reach pandemic proportions."

"Okay, what does that mean for us?"

"If it is judged to be a pandemic, then I reckon they'll close the borders, forbid people to travel in and out of the country indefinitely, and perhaps isolate everyone who isn't working in essential industries."

I watched Jamie carefully. Something was on his mind other than this illness, and suddenly the penny dropped. "You want me to go back to Jomtien for evaluation now instead of waiting the full twelve months."

"Yes, mate, they're asking for you so they can complete the assessment, but given the virus situation, I certainly wouldn't force you. I couldn't do it."

"How long would they need me?"

"About a week."

"If I don't go, what would happen to the program?"

"To be honest, we'd probably lose our funding temporarily and have to reapply. That would put us back where we started. You were the first patient in Victoria to have this treatment, and your success has been stunning. The drug court, through Judge Beecroft, as you know, facilitated the process with a light sentence, provided you took advantage of the treatment. All we have to do now is to allow Resort Jomtien to evaluate your results and provide both a written and video report. As it has turned out, almost all the patients from other states and territories have had good results also, but yours has been the first, the best, and certainly the most political for Victoria."

I smiled at my future stepfather; he was piling on the bullshit, but I knew how much this meant to him and in turn to Mum. There was no chance he'd ever put me in the way of harm via the virus, but the elephant in the room hadn't been mentioned.

"Look, Benny, this will work out. Matt will be back in your life sooner rather than later, I'm sure. In any case you'll only be away from home ten days at the most, and if he tries to contact you, we'll be here to assure him of your prompt return."

THE THAI Airways flight was only one-third full. I was depressed sitting by myself—going to Thailand last time I had Jamie with me, and coming home, Matt was by my side.

"Good afternoon," a voice spoke, and I turned to see a handsome "trolley dolly," as Matt would've described him. "Why don't you find your bags and follow me," he said quietly, leading the way forward and indicating a plush-looking seat in Business Class. "I thought you looked a little lost, so we've upgraded you."

"Thank you so much," I said, knowing there was a massive difference in the comfort factor of Business versus Economy, without even considering the food, which was supposed to be stunning. I reflected on human kindness; how one person, through a simple act, could make another person feel better about themselves, and how Matt would've enjoyed it if he'd been with me.

My new friend had all the amazing Thai good looks and beautiful manners without appearing servile, and for a while I forgot about my troubles. He was attentive and understanding, and after dinner was cleared away, he sat with me. I felt like a fool—I blurted out my life story, and to my amazement, I found a kindred spirit. Rama was the middle child in his family, his father had been killed in a tractor accident on their farm near Chiang Mai, and he'd worked hard to put himself through college. He, too, had always thought of himself as heterosexual, although he enjoyed "playing" with boys and even ladyboys, "as most Thai men do."

"Then," he said, "I met Gavin, an English pilot working for Thai. He was very lonely. His wife run off with another man, and he wanted to get away from the UK. We became very close friends and managed to get two weeks of annual leave together—at Phuket. He was very shy and,

ah, introverted, but I soon fixed that. We fell in
love, but Gavin couldn't believe it could happen
to him, and suddenly he is being fucked by a man,
so he called it all off, and I think both of us very
sad. Three months later there is a layover in Melbourne, and he had next room to mine, but I tell
him he has his room as a dressing room. He use
my room as the undressing room!"

I laughed at Rama. He made everything sound
so simple, which indeed it was.

"So where is he now, Rama? Do you work
together?"

"Second officer," he said, pointing to the
locked door. "Thai Airways decide much better
for family harmony if we fly together."

"They sound quite progressive," I said, "but
what happens if everyone is quarantined with this
virus?"

"All good. We are starting family. I have cous-
in who is very poor, already have many children,
and she is pregnant again about five month. He
will be our number one kid. We go up to Chiang
Mai and live there until flying again."

Suddenly I forgot my blues as I listened to
Rama. Not only did they seem an unlikely couple, like Matt and me, but they'd got through all
that sexual orientation process, and against all
odds they were planning a future together. We'd
come through the process, but one partner wasn't
sure—not whether he loved me or not, but because he thought I'd charge off with a female. I
cursed my lost opportunities of not speaking up
when I should have done. I nodded off, despite

an interesting movie, my body telling me I needed to catch up on sleep. I was nudged awake by
Rama with a toilet pack, and I made my way to the
washroom to freshen up, then returned to my seat
feeling wide-awake. I'd hardly buckled up again
when he appeared with a guy in gold braid, about
ten years his senior, with steely gray hair fashion-
ably styled, wonderful blue eyes, and an unlined
face, looking impossibly handsome.

"Ben, this is my Gavin, and this is Ben O'Connor," he said, smiling at his partner.

"Welcome back to Thai Airways," he said.
"I trust the cabin staff have seen to your every
need?"

"If they attended to all my needs, you'd probably throw me out at ten thousand meters."

He laughed heartily, slapping his thigh and
grinning at Rama. "He does have a way with
words, doesn't he?"

"He does. We all need a good laugh these
days."

"How long are you in Thailand?" asked Gavin.

"A week or so, but I'm thinking of cutting my
visit as short as possible—this virus seems to be
spreading faster than anyone thought."

"Yes, you're wise. We think we'll be ground-
ed within the next two weeks, so you need to book
your return flight no later than tomorrow."

A tingle of panic tickled my tummy. These
people were closer to the eye of the storm than
me, and I needed to balance my responsibilities
with my personal safety. I thanked them both for

their hospitality and kindness. Gavin shook my hand and returned to the cockpit.

"May I have your phone, Ben?" Rama asked, and a minute or so later we had each other's numbers. "I have texted you our forward schedule. It would be lovely if you are on one of these. Now, lovely man, buckle up. We're landing in twenty minutes."

Chapter 42
RETURN TO JOMTIEN

A NICE-LOOKING Thai lady with my name on a placard directed me to wait at a door at Suvarnabhumi Airport as she phoned my driver. She and I were almost knocked over by a Toyota Commuter bus that had probably seen better days, and to my horror, it was my transport.

"I am Chakan," yelled a fiftysomething bloke, seizing my bag and literally throwing it in the back of the vehicle, then slamming the rear door with a thunderous bang.

I turned to the placard lady, but she'd conveniently disappeared, so I resigned myself to an uncertain fate, stepped inside, and buckled my seat belt. The first thing he did was to drive over a curb to make a shortcut, and I lost it.

"Slow down and drive properly, you prick," I yelled, literally fearing for my life.

"Is okay. We get home soon."

"Don't fucking drive like that or I'll jump out," I roared, noticing the maintenance was so bad I could open the sliding door while he was driving. I kept my seat belt on but pulled the door wide open and was rewarded by a look of fear on his face. "Now slow down and drive properly or I jump." I had to shout to be heard above the wind noise.

Immediately he lifted his foot, and I slowly closed the door. He sulked, and despite my efforts, declined to speak further, which was irritating given the attitude of most Thai people, who are always gentle, warm, and welcoming. This one was a stupid cunt.

We stopped for a toilet break after about fifty minutes, and I gratefully had a nice leak, then stretched my legs. There was a convenience store next door, and I bought two ice creams—one for me and one for my driver, assuming anyone could possibly classify him in that category.

"For me?" he said disbelievingly and took it almost reverently, as if he couldn't believe the enemy had offered him an olive branch. Except I wasn't the enemy—a paying customer, no less. He stuck the ice cream temporarily in the bin between the front seats and gave me a grateful wai, which I returned. Our trip resumed as he kicked the little diesel over, and we drove on almost sedately until we neared Pattaya. The farther we went, the more obvious it became that he was absolutely lost. We were driving around and around all the knock shops and bars of Pattaya, fifteen minutes away from Resort Jomtien.

"There," I said, knowing he'd missed the bypass road entirely. "Follow that tuk-tuk."

I'd spotted the parking area for the one-ton vehicles, so I knew exactly where I was and directed him. He had no GPS, no idea, and no hope, and he was amazed when I directed him up the driveway of Resort Jomtien.

"This no hotel!" he bellowed.

"No. Hospital," I said, "for sick cunts like you. Why don't you book yourself in."

He shook his head that it was all too much for him as he handed me what was left of my bag. I felt a need to not see him again, so I gave him one hundred baht in the hope he'd disappear, and he did, very nearly sideswiping the gatepost as he left.

IT WAS quite late at night, but Mae was still hard at work. She flew out from behind the desk, giving me a lovely smile and a deep respectful wai. "Mr. Ben, so beautiful you come back. You been a good man, no drugs?"

"I am a good man, Mae. No drugs."

"That's what we think—you be good. Come, you go to your old room."

My head spun with the memory of hearing Matt crying that night, and I had difficulty keeping up with Mae, who seemed totally unconcerned that I was here by myself, the teamwork of Matt and me nowhere to be seen. We stopped outside my open door and switched on the light. Glancing at the closed door of what had been Matt's room, I started to sniffle a bit but decided I was being stupid and should pull myself together. The last thing

Jamie Weiss needed was the inference that while patient O'Connor wasn't using drugs, he seemed to lapse into emotional collapse frequently.

There was a light under the door and the sound of muted voices. I hoped whoever was in Matt's room was decent and quiet; I needed a good night's sleep. I left the door open as I unpacked, my claustrophobia exerting itself, as it did sometimes when I was tired. The door opened in the next room, and I recognized Ross's voice. I strode across the room to say hello, because he was still one of my favorite people. Then I stopped, rooted to the spot, my ears pricked up like a kelpie. The other voice—the intonation, the way he pronounced his words—was unmistakable. I sprinted past a grinning Ross and into the arms of the only person I have ever loved. His response was as startled as mine, but his grip on me was even more determined. Neither of us was ever letting go again, because we loved each other. The world could go and fuck itself. I had my bloke back, and I wasn't giving him up.

Chapter 43
FULL SPEED AHEAD

THE DOOR clicked behind Ross, and our clothes flew through the air, our lips never losing contact. There were a few "I love you" words, but the sheer sexual tension was overwhelming. For the first time, sexual intimacy was a communicator for the way we felt about each other, and it was so because we were making love. The final link had slipped into place as we spun around in the sixty-nine position, our orgasms following in a rush and within a blink of each other. We lay in each other's arms, still gently kissing, and despite our exhaustion, running our hands over each other, as if our fingers were remembering and retracing the bumps and valleys of our bodies, becoming reacquainted with each other, the two becoming one again.

Matt looked at me, determined to have his say, raising himself onto his elbow and eyeballing me. "I'm so sorry, Ben. I must have put you through hell. You talked to Will, didn't you?"

"Yes, I talked to Will, and no wonder you freaked out. I'm as much to blame because I couldn't get the words out. At the time, you see, I was all prepared."

"Prepared?"

"Yes. Wait there, don't go away."

"I wouldn't dare," he said, smiling, as I pulled on my underdaks and went next door. I came back with the little black silk bag with a drawstring.

"I've carried this with me every day," I said as my beautiful bloke looked puzzled. "I was going to present it to you the night before you left, but I chickened out, knowing I'd probably get rejected. But I think my chances might be slightly better now. What do you think?"

He was either being thick, which wasn't like him, or a touch overcome, so I knelt by the side of the bed in my undies and said, "Matthew Wilson, will you marry me?"

I opened the bag, and two rings sparkled in the light from the bedside lamp. I watched the expression on his face change from shock through acceptance and then pure joy as he bounced up, kissing me on parts of my body where I'd never been kissed before.

"Yes, of course I'll marry you," he breathed, smiling so his face nearly split in half. "Ben, you're amazing. I feel more guilty than ever now, walking away from that."

"But you weren't ready, were you?" I said.

"No, I wasn't ready, mainly because I thought you were still in denial, but I am now, because I know you love me. Well, I love you, Benny. I always have."

"And I love you too."

Chapter 44
THE FIRST DAY OF THE
REST OF MY LIFE

THE LIGHT woke me. In this part of the world, it was hard to disguise the dawn; it was as sudden as dusk. Morning breaks very quickly near the equator, like switching a light on or off. But waking like this was my idea of heaven, like when we first met and shared a bed. I'd had the most amazing sleep, and I somehow knew he had too.

I felt him stir, and I copped a wet kiss on his ear. This was no ordinary day—it was our first morning as a couple, after all. But there was something extra this morning I'd forgotten about; the feeling of oneness that was Ben and Matt, the feeling that had cured our addiction and rebuilt our minds, returning us back to the world as functioning people on exactly the same wavelength. It was so strong now I actually knew what he was thinking.

"You're going to tell me what happened after you left and how you came back here to Jomtien, aren't you?" I said.

"Yes, exactly. We still know what's going on in each other's heads."

He smiled that beautiful bloody smile, and I nearly melted in his arms.

"Well, I went back to Sydney and stayed in a hotel near Darling Harbour, trying to keep out of the way, but I couldn't settle. I knew what I'd done to myself. I felt guilty as hell about leaving, but seeing Jake's name on the door at Waratah freaked me out. I tried forgetting it, but I couldn't. All these years later I'd never forgiven him for what he did to me, but stupidly I put you in that category as well. In my anxiety you were another straight bloke about to break my heart. To keep myself busy, I went to Michael Parker's office to discuss my finances, I wasn't there ten minutes when he put the moves on me, and that was the final straw in my anxious state of mind. I told him to fuck off and never to come anywhere near me ever again. I was so mad I was in tears. There was only one person I wanted to be with, and it certainly wasn't him."

"He obviously didn't want me around. I'm not his favorite person."

"Because you were competition, darling," he said.

I'm his darling now; how cool is that?

"Well, I went to my legal people, and they arranged to transfer everything away from him into a safe place, until we can decide how to invest it or use it for whatever purpose."

"But that's your money. That shouldn't concern me."

"Do you know what Queen Isabella of Spain said to Ferdinand of Aragon before they married?"

"Enlighten me."

"'What's mine is mine and what's yours is mine as well,' and that applies to us both. I insist our accounts, as soon as possible, are merged—because that's the only way we can work successfully. A couple should share everything they possess when they decide to join their lives together. It's called trust, and that's probably our greatest strength, don't you agree?"

My head spun with the revelation, but I knew if the tables were turned, I would have done exactly the same. I smiled. "Yes, I agree, and thank you. We'll sort that out when we get home. But you still didn't explain how you were here at the same time as me. Were we set up?"

"Yes, partly. After the fiasco with Michael Parker, I went to my old GP in Sydney. I hadn't seen him since John's passing. I told him everything, the drugs, the chemsex parties, the treatment here in Jomtien, and of course meeting you. It helped he's a gay man as well, and I explained my dilemma—being terrified of a relationship with a straight guy again, and the realization that not only was I still in love with you, but I loved you more than I'd ever loved anyone in my life, and that included my late husband. That stopped me in my tracks. I'd verbalized what had been on my mind ever since I took off. The old doc agreed I'd had all the holistic treatment here in Jomtien, which had worked extremely well, but it was time

I had some simple modern medication to control my mood swings, so he put me on some mild anti-depressants, and I haven't looked back."

"Jesus, what did you do then?"

"Well, I talked to Will, who told me I was a silly queen and that you and I played for the same team anyhow. Will reckoned you sounded lovely, and I'd better get my arse into gear before anyone else snaffled you up. But I still felt embarrassed, the way I treated you and your family, so I thought a week or so at Jomtien with Ross would give me the confidence I needed to contact you again. I called Ross, and he went into the stratosphere, begged me to get on the first plane I could because the Commonwealth Health Department were here inspecting the place and I was a walking credential for them. I didn't know you were here until you walked in."

"So Ross and Jamie have been matchmaking. What did you think when I walked in the door?" I asked with a smirk.

"I knew it was meant to be, so I let the hand-brake off."

Chapter 45
A MOMENT IN TIME

WE LAY there kissing, lost in each other, our tongues gently exploring together, awakening the rest of our bodies, Matt deftly swinging over on top of me, our lips never losing contact. Our eyes smiled at each other as the morning sun drove the light brighter in the room.

Suddenly there was a banging on the door that nearly split the panels in half, and a voice which could only be Ross in his most homespun and outrageous manner. "Wakey, wakey," he roared, "hands off snakey!"

Matt flew off me, our erections disappearing like ice on a hotplate as the door cracked open. A grinning Ross led the way, followed by Kit and Aran.

"Breakfast in bed for those who need all their strength," he said, as he placed the big tray on the desk at the end of the room. Kit had a pitcher of fruit juice and Aran a carafe of coffee. We lay there under the sheets, trying desperately to retain a modicum of modesty as Kit pointed to the mound in my pubic region.

"Snake," he giggled.

"Cobra," said Aran, pointing at Matt's display, which was beginning to stand to attention again.

We all laughed. "Thanks for the brekky," I said. "Where do I sign?"

"You'd better ask Matt," Ross said with a laugh. "Looks like he's got more lead in his pencil."

"Do you do this for all of your customers?" Matt asked.

"No, only the slutty ones like you two. If you keep up that nightly performance, you'll pass away, and we can't have that."

"Well," said Matt, trying to look offended but not succeeding, "I'll have you know we're not slutty—two healthy fiancés getting in some practice."

Ross stopped as we held up our fingers with the rings glinting in the sunlight, and he bellowed with joy, dragging out his phone and running from the room, followed by the boys. Our news would be old news before we knew it—in the nicest possible way. Yod would certainly be here within the hour, so I jumped up, locked the door, and resurrected our undies and bathrobes. I vaporized my breakfast, and Matt ran a good second place.

"It's touching, isn't it?" Matt said.

"Wha-?" I replied with a mouthful of scrambled egg.

"They've remembered our favorite foods after all this time, even how we like our coffee."

I realized they'd done exactly that. With our laid-back attitudes, Australians and Thai people were so compatible; we liked each other, and we understood each other. The simple things in life were important to us both.

WE FINISHED breakfast quickly. My second coffee sat on the bench while I showered, Matt walking in behind me. I contemplated some hanky-panky, but both of us were aware we had a job to do for Ross and Jamie. Only then could we focus on ourselves before flying home.

"I think we should be ahead of the game," I said. "This bloody virus thing is looking pretty serious around Asia. Some friends from Thai Airways gave me their flight schedule and said we should try to catch a flight they're on. The last flights to Melbourne out of Bangkok will be next week sometime, so I think we should book seats now."

"I agree. I'll help you in a moment. In the meantime I have a phone call to make."

"Oh, I'll leave you to it."

"Benny, I need you to participate, okay?"

It was lovely to have someone organizing our life instead of me leading the family group as I'd done in the past. He dialed the number with his phone on speaker, smiling at me as my son answered, "Peter O'Connor speaking."

"Is that *the* Peter O'Connor, the good-looking intelligent young man who—"

"Matt!" Peter yelled. "Where are you? Dad's been looking for you everywhere, and we've all been so worried, and please tell me where you are so we can tell Dad."

"Dad's here already, mate. That was quick, wasn't it?" I said.

"Dad, what's going on?"

Matt held my hand. "Is it okay if I tell him?"

I nodded. The emotion had caught up with me, and I knew what Matt was on about.

"Pete," he said, "how would you like another father?"

"But I've already got Dad, and you too if you come home again."

"Well, I am coming home, but can you keep a secret?"

"What's going on?"

"Well, Dad asked me to marry him, and I said yes, so you'll have two real dads forever. Is that all right?"

There was a stunned silence and then yelling as he ran, obviously with phone in hand. Then he was babbling incoherently to Mum.

"Hello," Mum said. "Who's this?" She didn't recognize the number, of course.

I took over. "Mum, it's me. I'm in Thailand, and I have Matt here with me, and yes, we're going to get married as soon as we get home and do all the paperwork."

Then I could hear Mia and Garry in the background, the noises they were making unseemly for a woman in advanced pregnancy and her usually fairly quiet mate.

"Now," I said to my other half, "are you convinced that everyone missed you and that you're welcome home?"

He smiled that beautiful bloody smile again, and my heart skipped a beat.

Chapter 46
THE UNSEEN DANGER

THE PLEASURE in Mum's voice was palpable. All her kids were finally with life partners she loved, and Matt's place in our family circle would be restored permanently. No more drugs, no more drama, and Peter would have two parents who adored him. But there was something else. I could feel it.

"What's wrong, Mum?" I said quietly.

"Ben, dear, things are moving much faster than anyone predicted. The Australian borders will be closed tomorrow, I think, which means only Australian citizens will be allowed in, and they will need to voluntarily quarantine themselves at home for two weeks. It appears we'll all be in lockdown here for goodness knows how long, to slow the spread of this disease. We'll have to stay at home, only allowed out for exercise, shopping for food, visits to the doctor, and work. Peter will have to be schooled from home. At all times when in public, we must stay one and a half meters apart from each other. This stuff is highly contagious; it's very easy to pass on."

A cold shiver flew down my spine as I met Matt's eyes. This was obviously dangerous, life-threatening stuff, and the measures taken at home in Australia were so unheard-of it was hard to believe. Matt's hand slipped around my shoulders to gently massage out the tension, and I felt his strength, his simple gesture of support reminding me we were in this together. We thanked Mum and ended the call as a knock sounded at the door. It was Ross, brandishing his phone with the speaker turned on, and we recognized Jamie's voice.

"Firstly, guys," he said, "its lovely to have some good news in the middle of all this mayhem. Congratulations to you both. Do I get an invitation to the wedding?"

"Only if you bring my mother."

"God, you're a bigger bitch than ever."

"Maybe we should warn Mary," Matt said. "You sound like you've changed teams."

The expression on Ross's face said it all; this was a reconnection with Australia. While he loved Thailand and had been adopted by Yod's family, he'd obviously missed the easy repartee of gay and straight guys taking the piss out of each other. "Jesus," he said, "what a bitch fight. All Mrs. Bowman needs to put us down further."

"Who is Mrs. Bowman?" Matt and I asked in unison.

"She's the dragon sent by the Department of Health to certify this place for Medicare," Ross said.

"Sorry, mate," Jamie cut in. "I had no influence in who they sent. Is she that bad?"

"Worse. She's a born-again Christian who hates everything we stand for. She doesn't understand why we use the monastery. She's convinced they're filling our patients' minds with evil and untrue Buddhist dogma."

"But they teach patients to meditate," I said. "Nothing to do with religion."

"Of course, but you try telling her that."

"Perhaps we should take her up to the monks for some education," Matt said.

"That's not a bad idea, Matty," Ross said. "Jesus freaks like her are mostly trisexual anyway. She could keep them entertained for hours."

Jamie chuckled as we stared at Ross. "Okay," said Matt, grinning away, "so what's a trisexual and how are they different to a bisexual?"

Ross looked at us with a straight face. "Well, she looks and sounds so frustrated, I reckon she'd try anything."

Chapter 47
A SURPRISE AT EVERY TURN

AT ROSS'S request we came to the dining room for coffee and pastries. A quite pretty-looking middle-aged woman in a business suit and severe hairstyle was seated with a laptop open, typing furiously away, with Ross hovering around her.

"Ah, Barbara," he said, "here are our honored guests from our first Australian intake, Ben O'Connor and Matt Wilson. Gentlemen, this is Barbara Bowman."

"How do you do," I said, mindful of Mum's teaching of manners, smiling while inclining my head.

Matt knew instantly it was holding-our-heads-high time, while exercising some old-fashioned manners that would probably make her feel inadequate. "Oh, how do you do, Mrs. Bowman," he said. "I hope you're not finding the weather too humid?" I thought he did pretty good for a boy from the western suburbs of Sydney. He could read my mind like a book.

Barbara Bowman responded with a version of "pleesed ta meetcha," and Ross's face turned a nice purple color as we smiled at her in a pleasantly patronizing manner.

I couldn't help but stare at her. She was familiar to me somehow, and her face and her mannerisms worried me. I simply couldn't place her, but intuition told me to be on my guard, because when I worked it out it probably wouldn't be a happy memory anyway.

"These two are our heroes," Ross said. "If we were running a college, these two guys would have graduated with honors. They became close friends and not only helped each other but set an example to the other patients. In every intake I always hope for one patient with a positive mindset. This time I got lucky with two of them. They reminded me of my partner and myself when we were in trouble, first in rehab and then in Chiang Mai in a similar place to this. We had a comparable effect on each other."

"And where is your partner now?" Mrs. Bowman asked. "I suppose she couldn't stand the pressure."

"No," said Ross. He appeared quite composed, but I saw the merest hint of stress as he clenched one hand, no doubt imagining how he could fit it around Mrs. Bowman's neck. "My partner is Yod, and he runs the most successful travel agency in Jomtien."

"Oh, I see," she sneered, with all the sensitivity of a bulldozer.

A polite knock at the door caused Barbara Bowman to frown as Por's smiling face appeared, followed by Kit and Arun. "Boss, okay we measure and do the marks?" Por asked.

"Yes, please, boys, as soon as you can, thanks."

"What's that for, and why are we being so rudely interrupted?" Mrs. Bowman snapped.

"In case you hadn't noticed, madam, the coronavirus disease is spreading so rapidly outside China that the World Health Organization has proclaimed it a pandemic, which in our case means Thailand is taking the risk to human life and society most seriously. This whole country will be locked down. We will continue to take local patients under strict social distancing and quarantine conditions, but alas, none from Australia until the risk diminishes or a vaccine is developed or both."

I thought Barbara Bowman's mouth would never stop twitching as she tried to find the nastiest remark possible, looking like a barracuda out of water, gasping as Ross established the priorities of Resort Jomtien and clearly put her business so far down the list she was out of sight. Her phone rang, and she answered the call with deference. We knew it had to be her boss.

"But sir," she whined, "my report would suggest otherwise. This organization is full of undesirable people, and they use a Buddhist monastery—" She wasn't able to finish; it was clear her boss was pulling rank on her. "Yes, sir, I'll pass that on, and I'm booked on tomorrow's morning flight. Thank you, sir." With yet another facial twitch, she addressed Ross. "I have been told your establishment has been awarded Medicare status, which will be effective as soon as this coronavirus disease has been eradicated and patients will be able to travel again. However, I want you to know my report will suggest otherwise. I have never seen such depravity and disregard for proper religious principles."

Suddenly it hit me. "Mrs. Bowman," I said pleasantly, "was perchance your maiden name Smithson?"

Her face lost its ruddy color. "Yes, why do you ask?"

"Is you brother's name Andrew?"

"Oh, poor Andrew," she said, "thrown into prison by heathens on trumped-up charges. But he's recently embraced the Lord, and he'll be re-born into the Christian family."

"My ex-boss," I explained to Ross and Matt, who looked even more surprised than his sister. "He's doing a long stretch as the guest of Her Majesty—" I paused to laugh because I couldn't stop myself. "—for having sex with minors and supplying them with drugs, helped by his boyfriend."

"My, my, Barbara, you do have an interesting family," Ross said. "We sound quite pedestrian by comparison."

"You nearly killed my brother with a car!" Barbara suddenly shrieked. "I recognize you now. You drove a car into his lovely real-estate business and severely injured poor Andrew. You should have been charged with attempted murder with life behind bars."

"You can't argue with the justice system, Barb. They sent me here instead. The Lord must have been watching over me, because my addiction was cured and I met my fiancé here." I pointed at Matt.

For the second time, Barbara Bowman was lost for words, and I felt sorry for her naiveté.

"Look, Barbara," I said, "your brother did some terrible things as a real-estate agent, in hindsight probably worse than the crimes for which he was convicted. He used to lecture me about the Eleventh Commandment."

"There's no such thing."

"Yes, there is, sweetheart. Thou shalt not get caught is the Eleventh, and he got careless and got caught. Enjoy your trip home."

Chapter 48
EXIT STRATEGY

MATT AND I worked through the questionnaire with Ross, completing the information that would tell the story of the first intake from Australia. Ahead lay a battery of blood tests and a complete medical to ensure there could be no mistaking our success: not only overcoming our addiction but demonstrating our much-improved cognitive function and changed character traits posttreatment.

"You have a dry sense of humor, Ben, that you didn't have before," Ross said kindly as I sat there, a little shocked. "You were a very serious fellow, focused on getting well again, but that image thing you had in your head back then has seemingly gone forever."

Matt smiled as if he knew all the answers, and he probably did, but Ross also had an observation on his character.

"Matt, you went from severely damaged goods to someone with purpose in his life again after you and Ben met, and even though you held back because of your view of his sexuality, you eventually became bossy and protective of Ben, taking responsibility for you both."

We laughed at each other, and my other half leaned over and gave me the gentlest, most loving kiss on the lips as our very insightful mate looked on, smiling.

JAMIE RANG again nearly two hours later, and this time there was a note of urgency in his voice. He began by apologizing profusely for putting us in the eye of the storm. "Even though," he confirmed, "the worst and potentially fatal cases of the virus have occurred mainly in senior-aged people with underlying medical conditions. I want you guys out of that place now. We miscalculated badly by sending you there, and I'm so, so sorry. Your mother would kill me if something were to happen to you guys. Besides, I gather Medicare status has been signed off anyway, so your visit was overkill."

"I wonder why the signoff happened so quickly," Ross speculated, his eyes twinkling.

"Oh, I understand the department had to clear the decks of all business so they could focus on the coronavirus," Jamie replied, "so they rang and asked me for my opinion, and I could only agree that Resort Jomtien was a highly effective and professionally run establishment. I explained that in Victoria we had at least sixty patients waiting, with an annual number of two hundred to process."

Matt pointed to the online reservations portal for Thai Airways, and I nodded. "Jamie," I said, "we're booked on the 5:40 a.m. flight out of Bangkok on Thursday, so we should be in Melbourne about 8:00 p.m. your time. You know what Immigration and Customs are like ordinarily. We could be another hour or so after we land."

"Yes, I understand, but now there's also two weeks of voluntary quarantine at home, not that it will bother you two lovebirds. You'll probably stay in bed all day."

"What a disgusting old man you are," I said. "Fancy thinking that of us. We'll be trying to make a contribution to society in a meaningful way."

"Like making face masks in the dining room," Matt said. "There's bound to be a shortage."

Chapter 49
HEADING HOME

WE BOTH felt quite fit. Our immune systems should have recovered from the onslaught of methamphetamine by now, but this was all new, so serious was COVID-19's potential to kill thousands of people. Italy and Spain were cases in point; hundreds were passing away every day, and it was getting worse. We watched BBC and CNN while the ABC channel gave us a glimpse of what was happening at home in Australia, where we appeared to be ahead of most Southeast Asian countries in readiness.

The situation in the UK and the United States was frightening, the numbers of infections seemingly out of control and with an uncertain future. China had stepped up their efforts in a very authoritarian manner, and regardless of what we thought of their way of life, it appeared to be working. The local population of Wuhan was in strict quarantine. But the images of people overwhelmed by the disease dropping in the street was unnerving, and we knew we had to be careful. Already we were practicing social distancing at Resort Jomtien, our Australian pie shop and bakery was closed like most other businesses, and the umbrellas and deck chairs along Dongtan Beach had been spirited away. When we went to check out the beach, we saw a sign proclaiming anyone frequenting the beach was liable for a one-hundred-thousand-baht fine and/or three months in prison, so we quickly returned to the resort.

Yod was working from the office at the resort, processing dozens of refunds and canceling travelers' itineraries every day. He looked tired and worried. His staff were already at home, two of them also processing cancelations, so every day was a loss maker. No new business because no one could travel anywhere, inside or outside Thailand.

Resort Jomtien had emptied out, leaving only a few Thais and German, English, and Russian locals remaining as we packed our bags. Ross and Yod had dinner with us in their quarters—we both felt a sense of achievement in that we'd wrapped up the project, but also saddened that our contact with Ross and Yod would be minimal until the virus had run its course or a vaccine was discovered.

"You can always stay here," Ross said as we executed a perfect wai each in lieu of a cuddle, the social distancing necessary to remind each other how real was the threat out there.

"I know we could stay," Matt said, "but our hearts are linked so much to our family back home and the responsibility we share, particularly for our son. We'd also like to get married as soon as possible so our financial affairs are protected."

"And because we want to," I added as he turned to me with a brilliant smile, "so I can keep you chained to the stove."

"What about the bedpost?" he said.

"Too awkward with some of my moves. I'm hoping you'll hang around of your own accord."

At 2:00 a.m. it was still pleasantly warm outside as we waited for our transport.

"You feel sad leaving?" I asked Matt.

"Yes, but our future isn't here. We have to move on together—you with your nursing, me as a stove bitch."

He made me laugh yet again. I thought how different I felt now compared to when I'd arrived, this time, at Resort Jomtien. A few days ago, I was tense, on edge, wanting to get the job done for Ross and Jamie, then get back home to keep looking for Matt, only to find the love of my life back where we first met. Everything had a rosy hue to it, I couldn't stop the smile that seemed to creep on my ugly dial, and regardless of the terror engendered by the coronavirus, I felt no fear, only confidence we'd get through it and be there to look after older people in the community, like Gloria and even my mum.

Suddenly the darkness in the street was cleaved with light, and a smart-looking green-and-gold Toyota Commuter swung into the driveway. It swept toward us, and I thought the gods must be with us, as it looked brand new and not the old rattletrap that delivered me here. This was a petrol-engined vehicle, and I heard the engine note alter as the driver changed gear. It swept around the sharp corner before the main entrance, and my heart nearly stopped. With the same crazy expression and a hyena laugh, Chakan, my previous driver, jammed on the brakes in a shower of gravel. Matt looked at me with one eyebrow raised.

"It's the same prick who drove me here," I explained. "He's a lunatic. I promise you this will be the ride of your life."

"Oh," said Matt, always thinking the best of people, "he can't be that bad."

"Okay," I replied with feeling. "You judge for yourself. If we get to the airport in one piece and on time, it'll be a bloody miracle."

I'm sure Matt thought I was not only being pessimistic but rude to poor Chakan, so he tried to engage him in conversation.

"You have a nice new bus," Matt said, and Chakan laughed maniacally.

"That went down like a lead balloon," I said as we had a jackrabbit start. "Please put your seat belt on, Matthew." I sounded like a parent, and to my relief he did so.

"What happened to your other bus?" I roared at Chakan.

"Him break."

"Break or broken, not brakes that slow you down or stop," I confirmed to Matt, who was beginning to understand we were indeed taking our lives into our hands.

"Drive carefully, Chakan," I demanded, "or I'll have your guts for gaiters."

It was clear he hadn't the faintest idea what I was talking about, but my tone alone plus our previous adventures should have given him a clue. He began whistling and driving in the wrong direction, so I screamed at him to stop.

"You silly cunt, you're lost again," I said as he threw his hands in the air. "Turn around. You're taking us to fucking Cambodia."

He screamed with laughter again, and Matt shook his head. He obviously now understood I hadn't been exaggerating and was, at last, on board with me. Finally, after a hair-raising U-turn, we were headed in the right direction.

At least we had plenty of time, I thought. The traffic was almost nonexistent at this early hour—mostly trucks and small vans going to market with squealing pigs, fluttering chickens, and kitchen hardware glinting in the lamplight. I think I dozed off; next thing I knew Matt was shaking me.

"Hey," he said, "I think we've missed the turnoff. The sign back there pointed to the airport, and we're still going straight ahead."

"Chakan, wrong road," I yelled over the engine noise.

"Go to airport, is good."

"Which airport?"

"Don Mueang."

"You silly bastard, the booking was for Suvarnabhumi, where you collected me last time." I watched as my words began to register on our dimwitted driver.

"Ooh," he said as he realized he'd fucked up again.

Matt was really pissed off and took over, his language very direct. "We need to go to Suvarnabhumi Airport immediately. How do you plan to get us there?"

Matt's menacing tone was too much for him. He slowed down slightly, then proceeded to do a U-turn over the median strip between the lanes.

"Hang on!" I roared as the Toyota flew into the air, landing with huge force on the concrete. The floor moved under our feet as the rear wheels scrabbled for traction, finally catching and driving us headlong into the opposite lane in front of a small truck. We were close enough to see the whites of the other driver's eyes, and he shook his fist at us as we cowered in the back.

Chakan floored the accelerator; we knew we could be running late by the time we reconnected to the correct route, so we didn't dare remonstrate. It was warm enough outside, but strangely our feet appeared to be even warmer, despite the air-conditioning, and we both smelled something like burning oil or the like. The heat increased under our feet, and we yelled at Chakan as smoke began billowing out behind the bus. Next moment, there was a dreadful banging noise underneath, followed by a screeching sound as the bus slowed down and ground to a stop.

"Bus broke," Chakan muttered as we jumped from the vehicle, taking our bags with us.

"Where on earth are we?" I said, mainly to myself as Matt studied his GPS.

"Look," he said, absolutely in charge and with me loving it, "we're still at least forty-five minutes away, even with reliable transport. Thanks to this guy's antics, we're already so late that unless we get a ride quickly, we'll miss our plane for sure." I struggled to keep calm as Matt asked our driver what he planned to do.

"I phone boss." He grinned. "He sleeping or fucking—no answer." Chakan broke into his best braying donkey laugh but stopped when he saw the look on Matt's face.

"So how do we get to the airport?" snapped Matt. "Why don't you ring us a taxi?"

"Taxi sleep also. No come."

I hoped never ever to be in my partner's bad books, because it was clear he was nearing the end of his patience, a new experience for me.

"So we have to sit here while you fuck about, and we miss our flight to Melbourne," Matt said, his voice rising. "Find us a ride, you silly cunt, or I'll throw you under the next fucking vehicle that comes along. You imbecile!"

Chakan decided that discretion was indeed the better part of valor and ran out onto the highway, waving his arms at anything with wheels. Most of them waved cheerily back while Matt contemplated murder. Finally, an old tuk-tuk hove into sight and stopped, blowing diesel smoke and leaning to the left on a suspension that had seen better days. Chakan chattered away in Thai, and the driver smiled evilly at us.

"Two thousand baht," he said through his betel-stained teeth.

"That's about a hundred bucks Australian," I calculated.

"Who cares, darl? At least every minute we travel, we'll be farther away from that prick, and that's all I care about at the moment."

We threw our bags into the back and climbed on, holding on to the framework of the little truck's canopy as our driver floored the accelerator. Chakan began running alongside us.

"Money!" he screamed. "Tip." He rubbed his thumb and forefinger together in the age-old gesture.

It was my turn. "You already have one," I said, pointing at our new driver, who I'd seen slipping a few baht to him.

Defeated, Chakan slumped his shoulders and walked back to his "broke" bus as we roared off toward Suvarnabhumi.

Chapter 50
AN EXTENDED HOLIDAY

ONE OF my memories of Asia, particularly Thailand, will always be of the toll booths, a line of little houses strung across freeways to collect money from travelers, some with attendants, some automatic.

The driver's assistant slid the glass open. "Baht," he said—obviously to pay our fee as we rocketed toward a booth. We slid to a stop, paid our toll, and were in second gear when a khaki figure with lots of braid stepped in front of us, holding up a gloved hand to stop us. Almost immediately we were surrounded by Thai military, nasty-looking guns at the ready in case we made a run for it. We were told to dismount, our bags were searched, passports and tickets inspected, and we were waved on, but not before we were told in perfect English by the guy with the white gloves, "Put mask on—now."

The procedure was repeated twice more, and as we sped into the airport precinct, a jet with the distinctive Thai livery roared overhead.

"I'll bet that was ours," Matt said.

I nodded. I was upset. I hated being late for anything, but in the wisdom of hindsight, we should have allowed at least another hour for our journey.

Matt read my thoughts again. "Don't beat yourself up, Benny. Who could possibly know an idiot would be entrusted with our transport? It's very un-Thai and very unlucky! Anyway, there are worse things than being stranded around here waiting for a ride home."

There was no mistaking the entrance hall. The military lined the road on both sides as we approached, the old tuk-tuk belching diesel smoke and leaning over like a drunken sailor. The lines of soldiers became tighter, funneling us toward the doors. Our passports and tickets were inspected again, our temperatures were taken, and we were directed to the Thai information desk. Once inside it became clear why the military presence was so obvious. Literally hundreds of Chinese tourists packed the entrance hall. Social distancing was impossible as they pushed each other around, vying for a place nearer the head of the queue. They were the Chinese nouveau riche, first-time travelers, lifeblood of Thai tourism but also a prime potential for infection with COVID-19, and they were returning home earlier than expected. I nearly threw up as one of the women, a sturdy creature with a ruddy complexion, strode over to a trash can, clearing her throat as she walked, grabbed the lid, and let fly with a huge dollop of phlegm. Matt held his sides as my stomach churned, pointing me toward the queue at the Thai counter. My phone beeped with a text. It was Jamie.

Your seats given away because of your nonarrival, please respond ASAP, where are you?

I quickly replied, *Transport vehicle shit itself, we missed flight, at Thai information counter in long queue.*

A young Chinese bloke tried to push in, insisting he would miss his flight unless he got to the counter *now*. Matt eyeballed him, and I didn't catch his exact response, but it was clear to anyone watching that his breed of intimidation had met a brick wall.

"Sorry, sorry," he said, bowing to us. He was quite tall for a Chinese person, but no match for a 188-centimeter Australian with a glance that could curdle milk at twenty paces.

Finally we were at the counter, greeted by an attractive Thai lady who seemed to know all about us. "Your embassy has been in touch," she said politely. "Only Cathay Pacific and Qatar Airways are offering flights to Australia, but I know those flights are fully booked. Your embassy people ask that you book into the airport hotel, and they will be in touch. They say please keep your mobile phone switched on and charged."

We thanked her, found the little hotel within the airport, and checked in. The rooms were tiny, obviously designed for overnight stays, but at least we were away from the mass of humanity currently moving through the airport. So many were coughing, there was no social distancing, and we knew we were in danger if we hung around there much longer. We set the alarm and tried to get some sleep. It was only ten in the morning, but it felt like we'd been traveling for days. We cuddled up and were asleep in seconds. I woke to this perpetual buzzing sound as Matt reached over me and answered my phone.

"Yes, it's Matthew Wilson here. I'm Ben's partner, a moment, please."

I struggled awake and switched on the loudspeaker as Greg Peters from the embassy introduced himself. "Look, guys," he said, "there are repatriation flights being planned by our government, but none are coming this way. I feel your best chance of getting back to Melbourne is through Hong Kong."

"Jesus, what's the alternative?" Matt asked.

"I don't think there is one at the moment," Greg said. "You may have a long wait in Hong Kong, but at least your names are on the Department of Foreign Affairs and Trade, DFAT, master list, thanks to some serious pressure from back home, so you'll eventually get back to Melbourne that way. But I certainly wouldn't waste time around here if I were you. Airlines will be ferrying tourists back to China for at least two weeks, and as I understand it, there's not a spare seat going to any Australian destination either."

We thanked him, showered and changed our undies, and found the Cathay Pacific desk, where our tickets were waiting. I nearly fainted at the cost, but Matt tapped his card and it all happened.

"Thanks, Isabella," I said quietly.

"That's okay, Ferdinand," he replied and grinned. "It's your money as well."

Chapter 51
HONG KONG

THE AIRBUS A330 was like a cattle truck—absolutely packed, not one spare seat anywhere, no food, only water, and looks of fear on the faces of the cabin staff. There were few Westerners, although it was sometimes difficult to tell nationalities in the sea of face masks. There were some very well-dressed Chinese people—"Probably Hong Kong residents," Matt said—but the balance seemed to be the unsophisticated "nouveau riche" who were determined to get home to mainland China by any means possible, and if that meant returning through Hong Kong, then so be it.

Matt evidently knew Hong Kong well. I'd never been there, but he was a seasoned traveler in Asia. "John and I came here when the Chinese first showed interest in his business," he said, "and we came back twice after that. It's a lovely place but with almost no hint of its colonial period left. This is Money Land Central now."

From the news channels, we knew Hong Kong was in political turmoil anyway, and it was no surprise that all transit passengers were herded off the aircraft like sheep by unsmiling police, much less friendly than those in Bangkok.

"My guess is those blokes are from the mainland," Matt whispered to me. "Smile sweetly."

About twenty of us were shown into a room with a predatory-looking woman in an army-style uniform taking our temperatures at the door. At the far end was a desk manned by several other people seemingly determined never to smile at anyone or anything.

"Better to be looked over than to be overlooked," I murmured to Matt, who laughed his deep, hearty laugh, earning us a stare of disapproval.

"Passport," snapped the guy who had waved us over. "Australia!" He practically snarled at us as we handed both documents over.

"Yes," I said, "we're traveling together."

We were both aware of the need not to cause our Asian friends a loss of face, even if it meant agreeing with them at times when they were wrong.

"Why you come Hong Kong?"

"Ah, we're in transit, sir, waiting for an Australian government repatriation flight next week," Matt said quickly.

"That not come here."

"We have the Qantas flight number, sir, if that is of assistance, and here are our seat allocations."

"You will go to this hotel, second floor, not leave room," he instructed, handing us a slip of paper. "You pay hotel for room and food before leaving, otherwise you go jail. Next."

MATT KNEW the hotel; he'd been there overnight and assured me it was less than five minutes' walk from the terminal, but our whole group of in-transit misfits was marched to a bus and ordered onboard by uniformed people with guns at the ready. A few minutes later, around ten of us were escorted to the doorway of the hotel, where hotel staff and more guards awaited us. We were first at reception, our temperatures were taken again, and we were allocated a room after registering.

"Gentlemen, welcome to the hotel," a voice beside us said, and the general manager introduced himself as Stephen Hoskins-Brown, an Englishman. "Professor Weiss has been in touch and asked if I could look after you. I'll make sure your linen is changed daily, and of course we'll pay special attention to your food, but you must understand you're in quarantine, and you cannot leave the room under any circumstances. To do so would put the hotel at loggerheads with the authorities and place you personally in great danger."

"Yes, we understand," I said, glancing at Matt, who nodded in agreement. "We're grateful for your assistance."

"We're amazed at the show of force here," Matt said. "Some are mainland people, aren't they?"

"Correct. They're brimming with personality, aren't they?"

We laughed with him; his sense of humor was lovely and de-stressing for us. It had been a long day, and we couldn't wait to shower, change, and eat something, even though we were literally incarcerated.

WE FELT establishing a routine was important. In the mornings we did our meditation first, showered, and then stood on the balcony as breakfast was delivered. Our maid was lovely, and we made sure she was tipped every day. We'd pack up the breakfast dishes, together with the bed linens and towels, give her a buzz, and within ten minutes she was there, dropping off new linens so we could make the bed. We were evidently the only room who bothered, but it kept the risk low of contracting the disease and gave us something to do. Each day we took turns cleaning the bathroom, and by then it was time for morning coffee and a call from the nurse to establish if we had any symptoms. We assumed in advance, like many couples, that our relationship would be tested by our isolation, but the first few days solidified what we already had. We never stopped communicating with each other, even without talking. A nod, a grunt, a silly smile, an arm around the shoulder or, more likely, a gentle

caress during our lovemaking was enough to remind us we were traveling in the same direction,
with exactly the same agenda.

I WOKE earlier than normal on the sixth morning.
I'd dreamed stupid dreams all night and felt warmer than normal, even adjusting the temperature of
the air-conditioning. Matt was sleeping peacefully
as I crept out of bed. I had an urgent need for the
toilet and made it in time, seeming to almost empty my bowels. I stood up, feeling light-headed, and
had to sit down again. Something had given me
severe diarrhea. I thought back to dinner last night,
which was quite innocuous—vegetable soup and
chicken salad because neither of us felt very hun-
gry. The urge returned, and I went again; the force
of it was frightening, and I called out to Matt. He
poked his head in the door and screwed his nose
up, which ordinarily would have been funny, but
the sudden evacuation of my bodily solids had left
me weak, headachy, and trembling. I felt like there
was a fire in my throat now, and started coughing
a deep, hollow cough with no resulting phlegm.
Matt threw me under the shower, quickly washed
me, dried me off, and helped me dress. We had a
thermometer with us, and Matt took my temperature, which was 38.9 degrees centigrade.

"Darling, you're really ill," Matt said. "I'm
calling the nurse."

I tried to stand up and protest because it was a
lot of fuss about nothing, and the last thing I saw
was the carpet rising up in my face.

Chapter 52
The Tragedy of COVID-19,
by Mary O'Connor

I FELT I needed to have my say, whether or not this manuscript ever gets published. That's why you're reading this chapter. Because I was about to be threatened by the most horrible thing any mother has to face—witnessing a child's passing while she is still alive. Ben was my firstborn, and there was always a special bond between us, which had become even closer as the years rolled by. I've never known anyone so young to be so unselfish and to accept responsibility as he's done. Most other kids his age would have walked away and had a life of their own, but not Ben. Even through the darkest period of his own life, he tried desperately to focus on his family before anyone else, even if at times he was hard to live with. I've always believed in him, as have his sister and his brother and his son. We made allowances for his drug use, knowing there was an inner strength there that we hoped would see him kick his ice addiction.

TO BE honest, I didn't want Ben to return to Thailand, even though completing the survey would have a profound influence on substance addiction treatment in Australia, returning users to productivity and saving lives in the process. Jamie and I both knew the coronavirus was deadly in senior-age people, while it appeared to have a much more manageable and far less dangerous effect on younger people with stronger immune systems. Ben was only twenty-eight, and Jamie persuaded me he'd be perfectly safe. Not that Ben needed my permission, of course, but these days Jamie and I were in each other's lives once again, and anything that affected our kids was always cause for mutual concern.

I can't remember ever feeling so happy as when Matt rang us from Thailand and announced that not only had they met up again, but he and Ben were getting married. Matt was not simply a wonderful addition to our family, he was also so right for Ben, and he almost instantly became part of our brood. I watched with amusement as they danced around each other, only to part temporarily while Matt sorted his head out. Ben was in love at last, and with it came a realization for us all that love was life's real driving force—not sexuality.

The first indication something was amiss was when they missed their flight from Bangkok. Jamie rang me in a slight panic but assured me they were okay and would probably fly to Hong Kong and wait there for the Australian repatriation flight, due in about a week. As both the boys were considered to be on government business, they'd be given priority. So we all relaxed, and they spoke to us almost every day, keeping abreast of the situation here at home.

Then I had that fateful phone call from Matt— Ben had contracted coronavirus and needed immediate hospitalization in Hong Kong. Matt also had symptoms, but they were relatively minor. My nursing training kicked in; why had Ben been affected so quickly and profoundly? Matt knew I didn't need the facts sanitized for any reason, so I heard every detail of how Ben had diarrhea, accompanied soon after with the more common symptoms of COVID-19: high fever, sore throat, and a deep dry cough. I rang Jamie, who by this stage was nearly catatonic with worry, so I used some language only the Irish can, to get him focused.

"Listen, Jamie, fucking hysterics will get you precisely nowhere fast. This wasn't your fault. Pull your finger out and get in touch with casualty at Queen Mary Hospital on Hong Kong Island, and surely we can get a progress report. You must have contacts in Commonwealth Health who'll know someone." I felt better because he actually laughed at me; we both needed something to distract us, and we had to think clearly, in the most productive manner, to help Ben and Matthew.

No one understands what a mother feels like, except perhaps another mother, when their child is staring death in the face, and that's how it appeared with Ben because his condition worsened so quickly. He showed no progress toward any recovery. In fact the opposite seemed to be the case. His treatment wasn't all that different to the covid ward in my hospital here at home, except he was placed immediately on a ventilator and was sedated so he was in an induced coma. Jamie had spoken to the medical team and relayed the information to Matt and me, but it seemed all downhill, some of his vital signs barely stable.

We were all looking for a needle in a haystack, something that would turn the fight in Ben's favor. Sadly, the nature of this disease demands isolation from all but those directly treating the patient—whether in Hong Kong or Australia or indeed anywhere in the world—adding to the frustration of the patient's loved ones.

I rang the only person I could trust to carry this awful scenario to a conclusion, one way or another. "Matt darling," I said, "it doesn't look good at all, but we all have faith in you to make whatever decision necessary if and when they wake him from the coma."

Chapter 53
FATEFUL DECISIONS – by
Matthew Wilson

I COULDN'T move from the hotel room because after the test result, I too was diagnosed with coronavirus, and even if that hadn't been the case, I wasn't allowed in the hospital anyway. In fact at this stage, I was still a transit passenger and Ben's "friend," not even his next of kin. But I wasn't going to give up that easily; I needed to marshal support and organize for the future, whatever it may hold. The last thing I needed to do was to sit around feeling sorry for myself. That was how I went down the road of ice addiction when my previous husband died. Now I'd been given a second chance at life, and even if Ben passed away, it wouldn't be without a fight to keep him with me. Of that I was determined.

A reminder of how seriously Hong Kong treated the coronavirus was seated a few meters down the hallway from my room. I opened the door, and he stood up immediately, giving the normal traffic cop stop sign with one hand, the other reaching inside his coat. I smiled politely and quickly closed the door.

The next thing I did was to ensure both our mobile phones were fully charged, as was my iPad, because I reckoned if Ben had any chance of survival, I had to get our experts at home talking to the doctors supervising him, giving him input from both areas of expertise. Communication would be the key. I did a conference call to Mary and Jamie, suggesting a second opinion to get the best possible help, and Mary recommended Eddie Chan, the infectious diseases specialist at her hospital who'd treated Ben when he was at his worst on ice. Jamie said he wasn't an epidemiologist, but that hardly mattered, because Eddie was treating patients in the covid ward daily and had a very broad, practical experience of the disease and the treatments that worked. My mind was in overdrive, trying to absorb the facts as they tumbled out.

"Chan," I said. "Is he Chinese?"

"Yes," Mary said. "In fact I think he came from Hong Kong."

Bingo! Within the hour we had Eddie hooked up on Zoom with Mary, Jamie, and me. Twenty minutes later Eddie struck pay dirt and was speaking in Cantonese to the physician in charge of the coronavirus intensive care unit at Queen Mary Hospital. A short time later, the ward had my number as Ben's partner, and I was given an update on his condition whenever I inquired.

A FEW days later there was a text on Ben's phone from Rama and Gavin, and I wondered who the bloody hell they were until I read further.

Where are you, Ben? Are you OK? Noted your seats given away, sorry we had to leave you in Bangkok.

I remembered them then, of course. Ben had spoken of their kindness on the flight from Melbourne, and he'd texted Rama to expect us on the flight after he confirmed the booking.

I texted back. In our current situation, the more resources we could muster, the better, even if Ben went home in a casket.

Hi its Matt, Ben's partner. We missed flight because of mechanical breakdown. Currently in Hong Kong attempting to catch Qantas repatriation flight. Ben very ill with coronavirus in Queen Mary Hspital.

The reply was almost immediate. *So sorry to hear, we are in Chiang Mai. If you need our help please contact us immediately.*

I'd hardly finished reading when my own phone rang, and it was Ross and Yod. "Jamie gave us the news. How are you holding up, mate?" Ross asked.

"I'm okay, but Ben is really, really crook."

"I know. How long has he been there?"

"Two weeks tomorrow."

"And his condition?"

"The best outlook is that his vital signs are reasonably stable. The worst is that they should be much improved given his age, and they're not."

"So there's been no communication between the two of you at all since he fell ill."

"Ross, he was semiconscious when the ambulance collected him. I do have good information through a Zoom hookup between Jamie, Mary, Eddie Chan, the QMH, and me. They evidently started medication straightaway, and he's been in an induced coma in the covid ward ever since."

"Matty, remember the special gift you two have. When you work together, you harness many times the mental strength of a solitary person. Yod agrees with me. Wait until he improves, however slightly, then make them wake him up."

Chapter 54
HELLO WORLD

I COULD see a light ahead of me; it grew brighter as I moved down a tunnel. The light beckoned me, and I knew I wanted to go there. It seemed warm and inviting, and I felt I'd probably see people I knew when I got there. I picked up speed as the tunnel walls started slipping past. Suddenly I heard a voice, a crystal-clear voice, and I knew who it was—Matt.

"You silly bitch, come back. Don't fucking leave me here by myself."

I found I couldn't speak. I tried to, but no sound came out of my mouth. What did he mean by "leave him," I wondered. My progress toward the light seemed to have stopped. It was still warm and comforting, and I knew I'd be safe there, somehow, but I was really pissed off that Matt couldn't come with me.

"Come back here, Ben," he said, and I found myself being spun around and flying out of the tunnel into another bright light, which hurt my eyes but still didn't stop me from grinning. That was fun!

There was a clear plastic-looking bubble around me and a cushiony thing around my bum and legs as I tried to straighten up. A smiling Chinese lady in protective clothing gave me some ice to suck on, and I managed a sip of water.

"Where's Matt?" I said in a rasping voice and received applause from other Chinese-looking people gathered around me, also in protective clothing.

They engaged in excited chattering and beaming smiles as the doctor—Dr. Tang, according to her name tag—fed me more ice and a generous sip of water.

"Matt?" I said, expecting him to appear around the corner since his voice was still ringing in my head.

"Your partner," she whispered, and I managed to nod at her. "Tomorrow morning after you have some food and we walk you a little bit—about midmorning—I think you may speak to him on phone."

I started trying to fill in the blanks, and the doctor smiled, knowing my poor mind was in catch-up mode.

"You were in the transit hotel with your friend when you collapsed, and you were brought here. This is the Queen Mary Hospital. You have been here for nearly four weeks in an induced coma. We woke you and nearly lost you completely, but you came back to us. Now you are here to stay. All your vital signs are normal for the first time, and the ventilator has been switched off."

I was tired, very tired. My throat and nose were sore from all the tubes and pipes, but they turned me around from my nearly upside down position so I reclined more comfortably on big pillows, continuing to breathe without assistance. My breath was a bit raspy sounding, but it was dry, no mucus discharge, which the nurses said was excellent. The next morning I was fed soft solids, some rice in milk, which I could neither taste nor smell. I wanted more, including a coffee, but all I got was giggles from the nurses and a gentle no from Dr. Tang. I heard her a few minutes later instructing the nurses again, then dozed off, only to be woken by a small Chinese male nurse who pointed down the hallway and said, "Bath." I was helped into a wheelchair, the drip still in my arm, and all modesty disappeared, with my gown neatly removed, as I sat on a toilet.

"Try," he said. "Push hard."

"Nothing," I croaked, as I let go enough wind to send a tsunami down Hong Kong harbor.

"Very good. Tomorrow you do nice poo."

For the first time since this happened to me, I laughed, and my helper caught the mood. He pinched his nose, grinning and waving his hand over his face. "You eat good lunch and dinner today, then you do big one tomorrow."

Back at my cubicle, Dr. Tang greeted me, pointing to the entrance, asking my mate and I to follow her. We left the covid ward, entered a lift, and suddenly I was in a private room with a view of Hong Kong Island and a corner of the harbor. There was an old landline telephone handset beside the bed which started ringing urgently. Dr. Tang answered it and turned to me with a smile. "Your partner, Mr. Matt."

Chapter 55
A TRULY GLOBAL PANDEMIC

WE SPOKE multiple times during the day, every day. It hurt that politics and the pandemic had conspired to keep us apart, even as we now both tested negative. But both of us were humbled that we'd been spared the fate of so many people around the world who hadn't survived, reminding ourselves that it was our partnership, the linking together of our hearts and minds, that spared us.

I was thrown into rehab by Dr. Tang, who insisted that I wasn't going anywhere, let alone on a nine-hour flight back to Australia, until I was fit enough to do so. I began eating more, but I still couldn't smell or taste the food, which was bloody annoying. Still, Dr. Tang was insistent. I needed to eat because the gym program was relatively strenuous. Lunch was back in my room, followed by a little nap if I was lucky. After that it was walking in the pool to tone up my leg and back muscle mass, followed by a few gentle laps.

On several occasions I began to feel really strong, only to fall back the following day. Without Matt urging me on, I could easily have thrown in the towel—the damage to my body through the period of physical inactivity while in the induced coma was profound.

I had a television in my room; I watched with horror as the wave of infection took hold back home in Victoria and caused the health system to be overworked to hell. Front-line medical workers themselves numbered among the many casualties.

My phone buzzed, and it was Matt, who had been watching the same program. "We can stay here in Hong Kong, which is relatively safe, or go back to Jomtien with Ross and Yod if home looks too scary."

"We couldn't do that even if we wanted to," I said, knowing he was trying to make things easier for me, but I knew we both needed simply to go home to Casa O'Connor, with all our mad mob surrounding us with love and laughter. Importantly, it wasn't all about us. We had Peter as a responsibility that I'd left with my mother for far too long.

"Look, I agree," Matt said, "but getting home won't be easy. There's more tests, and two weeks quarantine in a nominated hotel, like a prison. Melbourne is besieged by the virus, and it sounds as if it's getting worse by the minute."

"Well, there is some good news. Dr. Tang seems to think I'm doing very well, and I agree. I reckon I've turned the corner."

"Oh?"

"Yeah. I cracked a stiffy this morning for the first time. That'll help pass the time in quarantine."

My partner, who was clearly mentally processing the possibilities, gave a throaty chuckle. "Listen, sexpot, has she talked about a discharge date, because I have to confirm arrangements, and I need nearly a week's notice to organize it."

"A repatriation flight?" I asked.

"No, it's a surprise."

"Oh, a commercial flight."

"No. Even with us now testing negative, they don't want to know about us."

"Oh, I understand, but what's the alternative?"

"When you find out, I promise you'll be delighted."

"Not a container ship calling at all ports."

"No, I told you, it'll be a nice surprise."

"I hope it didn't cost too much."

"No, Ferdinand, it was a wise investment."

"Okay, Isabella, I'll take your word for it."

Chapter 56
MELTDOWN

I WAS having a bad day. Yesterday I did far more in the gym and the pool than I expected and could have done even more, yet today I felt as flat as a pancake and went backward—no energy, no spark, no fucking nothing. Dr. Tang told me not to worry, that covid affected different people in different ways, and feeling exhausted was normal. The bloody jury was still out as to why the virus nearly killed me while in my twenties. No bastard seemed to know or care, and I felt anything but normal. I'd had two more tests since leaving the covid ward, and both were negative, so what was fucking wrong with me? It really pissed me off that I was cool as shit one day and fucked the next. I looked at myself in the mirror and hardly recognized the bloke looking back. I was fucking sad all the time, like some bastard had shot my dog—and I don't even own one.

The phone rang. Matt. "What sort of a day are you having, darl?" he said, and I launched into him.

"Don't you get it either?" I shouted. "No prick seems to understand I need to get out of this fucking place. I test negative, and yet you bastards all expect me to climb fucking mountains and be fit enough to run a marathon before I can get discharged. No prick cares about how I feel, period."

"Ben, you have to be fit enough to travel, and that should be next week sometime. You're actually doing quite well."

"Oh, here we go again, the big fucking secret. How are we going to get home to Australia? On a magic fucking carpet, I suppose?'

"No. I haven't finalized it yet. I should be able to give you the good news in about three days, with luck."

"Luck!" I screamed. "I'll make my own luck. I'll find my own way back, and you can enjoy all your own bullshit." There was something else I wanted to talk to him about, but the connection had been cut. I dialed his number, but it went through to a message bank. Then I dialed my own mobile, and that did the same, so I was royally fucked. All I had was the antiquated landline beside my bed, and no bastard wanted to listen to me. Why would they? I was Ben the Loser.

I started to calm down, realizing I probably didn't have a partner anymore after my outburst—because that's what it was, a stupid uncontrolled outburst from yours truly with shit for brains. I lost my cool, and my mouth took over. I'd always been a bit like that: quick to anger and take offense, like my father, and now it had come back to haunt me. It had probably cost me my only real chance to live a happy life. No partner could tolerate that sort of behavior for even the short term, let alone a lifetime.

I dozed off on the bed, exhausted again. I'd done my exercise penance for the day, and I felt rooted as a result. I dreamed lovely dreams of Matt and me walking around a bloody garden, or something similar, and he'd smile at me as he took my hand in his. Then he let it go with a sorrowful look on his face and disappeared. I was terribly upset, and I cried because wherever I looked, he wasn't to be seen, and I thought maybe I'd never see him again, ever.

I woke up to my body being shaken; it felt like an earthquake was in progress.

I opened my eyes as Dr. Tang stared at me, wiping my damp face with a sterile tissue. "You have been up and down for a few days, Mr. Ben. Tell me your worries, please."

"It's the same stuff I've had all my life," I replied. "I've got a quick temper. I'm often unhappy. I always felt I wasn't good enough, so I needed a pick-me-up. I think that's why I was addicted to methamphetamine."

"Yes, I agree, but why are you so sad today and crying?"

"Because I snapped at my partner. I was a dick, and I said things I didn't mean. He's pissed off, and I don't blame him. He won't return my phone calls, and I think it's over." I snuffled again as the bloody tears ran down my face like a waterfall.

"You have depression—mild case, I think. I will prescribe simple daily medication for you."

I paused for a moment; in the middle of my misery, this brilliant, cherubic-looking lady had shown me compassion and kindness well beyond her duties as a medico, and I struggled to understand why.

"Look, Doctor," I said, "you've brought me back from the brink of death, supervised my recovery, and you've spent an inordinate amount of time on me and my health, for which I'm very grateful, but there may be other patients here that require your help more than I do."

"You not able, as you Australians say, to piss me off that easily."

In spite of my predicament, I laughed at her, and her eyes danced behind her blue-framed spectacles.

"There are plenty of well-qualified medical staff to handle all emergencies. I concentrate on you for very good reason." I sat there as this little lady managed to put almost everything in my life back into perspective. "My husband is thoracic surgeon upstairs," she said, pointing heavenward at what must be the operating theaters. "We come from Xian in China, very much a scholar's city but also very traditional Chinese population. We want to give our son a better chance in life because he is gay boy like you and Mr. Matt, and to have relationship in Xian is very hard, almost impossible. My brother was same. He take his own life because he was so depressed, no place or time for him to be happy."

I quickly understood and tried to say how sorry I was, but she held up her hand and went on. "That is now past. He is with his ancestors. What is important now is your story. I have your file from Professor Weiss and Dr. Chan, and I talk to Mr. Matt and your mother. Australians are so fortunate. You can marry, have children, and be happy. Much improvement in attitude here, but our family will move to Taiwan or Australia if Hong Kong become too much like mainland."

My mouth fell open. My doctor certainly knew more about me than I did—which actually made me feel better in a way, because I probably wouldn't be alive if she hadn't pulled my files and spoken to all those closest to me. I suddenly felt a real bloody heel for my attitude and apologized.

A knock at the door announced a nurse with the medication; the prescription had been filled while Dr. Tang and I were talking. "Here," she said, "one tablet now and one every second day for the next five days, then one every morning. It usually a week before you notice difference."

"How long will I need to take them?" I asked.

"Forever." She smiled at my shocked expression. "Your genetics make you predisposed to depression, but coronavirus has some strange aftereffects with some patients, and that in my opinion is what has triggered your unhappy state of mind."

I dropped my head into my hands. "What am I going to do about Matt? I don't feel like I can go on without him."

"Ring his phone."

"But he won't answer."

"Ring phone, you silly boy."

I grabbed hold of the old instrument beside the bed, got an outside line, and then dialed his number. He answered almost immediately, which shocked me. He sounded as if he was in the next room, and I told him so.

"You could say that," he replied as the door opened and he walked in, his phone still to his ear.

"You have thirty minutes, Mr. Matt," Dr. Tang said. "Make the most of it. Make him happy boy again." She giggled, closed the door, and was gone.

It was like Jomtien. We made eye contact, and I fell in love all over again. His smile was so broad I'd swear his mouth nearly touched his ears as we fell into a long, lovely kiss, cuddling on the bed.

Chapter 57
WINGS ON MY FEET

THE HOTEL limo was waiting at the side door. If I'd hoped to make a quiet getaway, I was mistaken. Dr. Tang was there with her distinguished-looking husband and handsome son; no surprise—he was a medical student. Chocolates didn't fare well in this climate, so Matt and I presented Dr. Tang and all the nursing staff who cared for me with fruit and flowers, both considered a luxury in Hong Kong. Hallways were full of floral arrangements, and there were literally crates of apples, oranges, plums, and grapes. No durian fruit, though, because while it tasted heavenly, it smelled like shit.

I felt as if I was floating; my strength had finally begun to return to stay, and I believed I was almost well again, certainly so much better than I had been a week ago. I'd often seen videos of surviving covid patients being applauded as they left the ward, but in my case the celebration was saved for my departure from the hospital side entrance. Matt and I were seen as celebrities, but it was our status as a couple that had all the nurses fascinated, so Dr. Tang said, and not my amazing recovery from the virus. They thought we were so romantic!

And perhaps we were. We were both aware that after a commitment of only a few weeks, we'd survived our first disagreement by way of my meltdown. More importantly, though, Matthew hadn't hesitated for a moment to care for me through my illness and work toward the next step in our future. And I'd grown up enough to understand that if the tables had been reversed, I would've done the same for Matt. It wasn't a lurid sex life that had so captured the collective imagination of our mostly female fan base at Queen Mary Hospital; it was the love affair of Ben and Matt, who weren't shy about showing affection for each other in so many ways. And that was yet another lesson for us.

STEPHEN HOSKINS-BROWN sat waiting in the limo, managing to look and sound very much the English gentleman, complete with a stylish linen face mask. He handed Matt the hotel invoice, and Matt passed it on to me. I grinned; Matt was making sure I was involved, but he needn't have worried. Coincidentally, we were now on the same medication, both of us calm and productive. The hotel invoice almost mirrored the hospital bill— no charge for accommodation, only food and beverage and laundry. The sole cost at the hospital was for pharmaceutical items. I shook my head in disbelief.

"Are you sure these are correct, Matt?" I asked.

He nodded and smiled. Silly politicians back home were stamping around doing their best to alienate our Asian friends, when we'd received such wonderful care and kindness. It was obvious to us where Australia's future lay, and we vowed to do what we could to return the favor in years to come.

We swung into a driveway at the airport, our papers were checked, and we drove into an area which was effectively behind the counter of Immigration. We said our goodbyes to Stephen and promised to return when it was safe to do so.

"When you do," he said, "you'll be staying with Li and I, not at the hotel. Now please look after yourselves and stay in touch."

"Li?" I asked Matt.

"His partner of twenty years or so. He's a lovely bloke. They have an apartment in Aberdeen."

I marveled at the level of organization—such different treatment to our arrival. We were obviously expected. A wheelchair was provided that I really didn't need but accepted so our hosts didn't lose face. The formalities were handled quickly, with much professionalism, and Matt wheeled me into a lift that dropped two floors and opened directly onto the concrete apron outside. A curious-looking business jet was parked there with its crew standing on either side of the steps. All of them were in civvies, as expected, but Gavin and Rama stood out. They were so handsome, and they were clearly in charge. These people, having met me once traveling from Melbourne to Bangkok, had talked to Matt via Zoom, offered their services, and were prepared to fly us back to Melbourne for the cost of fuel and wages for the copilot and a nurse. The little aircraft was about to be retired from Thai Airways' fleet but had plenty of serviceable hours left. What helped was that Gavin had qualified with hundreds of hours on this aircraft, and a good friend, Sarawut, similarly as copilot. In case my condition worsened, Nam, a family friend from Chiang Mai, was my nurse. When the financial proposition was eventually put to Matt, he agreed as long as Gavin and Rama also pulled a wage for the flight. I was pleased, but not surprised, that Matt had done exactly what I would have insisted on had I been consulted. Deal done. Their son was due in a few weeks, so they needed to get the show on the road.

Chapter 58
TERROR AUSTRALIS

BECAUSE OUR aircraft was originally designed for short-haul service, we dropped into Darwin to refuel. It was a rough little bastard, short takeoff and landing characteristics part of its design. Gone were the relatively smooth landings of the normal commercial planes; this little thing seemed to fall out of the sky rather than land. Touchdown was crash down, no matter who was at the controls, but it was lovely to be on Australian soil once again. The local airport kindly allowed us to stretch our legs in the transit section, but that was it. Darwin, with its small population, had covid infection numbers at zero, but they were taking no chances on us. We were warned not to go any farther. I felt relatively well, but we still had six hours of flying remaining, and I was beginning to tire. Little Nam was adamant. As soon as we were airborne again, I'd be put to bed in a makeshift cabin arrangement with Matt close by.

A lemon-scented cloth brushed my face, Matt tending to me.

"About three hours to Melbourne," he said as Rama busied himself with a meal. I did feel refreshed. Thankfully, my sense of smell and taste were returning more each day, and my appetite with it.

"What's for dinner?" I asked, and Rama smiled.

"I think if his stomach is working then his dicky bird working soon," he said to Matt.

"Don't worry, it already is."

"Ah, but the quickest way to a man's heart is through his stomach," a voice boomed from the front of the aircraft as Gavin joined us, "and you're feeding him again. He'll be sex mad by the time we get to Melbourne."

We laughed together, naturally and easily for friends that had fallen in together by chance. Matt and I were keenly aware that the extraordinary circumstances of coronavirus had, in our case, prompted great kindness, bravery even. Gavin and Rama didn't hesitate to help us, to even risk catching the disease themselves. What we were flying into at home in Victoria was like flying into the eye of the storm. There were hundreds of infections daily, and many deaths, mostly elderly people from nursing homes, but my experience alone suggested different strains could have a mortal effect on younger citizens like myself. The state was going into lockdown again. We'd made it back to Melbourne before all incoming flights were to be canceled and diverted elsewhere. We had two weeks of quarantine ahead in a city hotel before we could return home.

"Are you still happy to do this?" Matt asked me as we finished a lovely meal of pad thai with chicken. "We could be at Casa O'Connor tonight with the family around us, doing our two weeks at home."

"Yes, we could, and it's nice to have that option, thanks to Jamie, but we'd never forgive ourselves if we've become reinfected and started another cluster at home."

"From what I've heard, the hotel thing isn't going to be a walk in the park either. There's been trouble with the security people. It's not like Hong Kong, where they knew what to do after the SARS thing a few years ago."

I knew Matt was right, but we'd also discussed the public perception of two ex drug addicts getting favorable treatment because we were deemed to be on government business, so we told an astonished Jamie we'd do our time in a hotel.

We actually touched down gently at Tullamarine Airport; it was as if we were tiptoeing to Melbourne's doorstep. We taxied in, pulled up at a nondescript entrance, and said our farewells to our amazing friends, who were staying over at the airport hotel until they were ready to fly home. If we thought we could sneak into the place undetected, we were wrong; we were certainly expected, but Immigration and Customs were done with us very swiftly, basically because the airport was almost empty. Restaurants were closed, lighting seemed to be at half power, the only signs of life were the security guards, who, like us, were all wearing masks. It was usual in Asia at any time, but at home in Melbourne, Australia, it was a grim reminder. The guards, male and female, formed a line on either side as we rolled our suitcases to an outside door. Once there, we were herded onto a bus together with about ten others, the door hissed shut, and we were bound for our hotel, a police car ahead and another behind. I looked at Matt, who raised his bloody beautiful eyebrows.

"Sort of makes Hong Kong look like a picnic, doesn't it?"

About thirty minutes later, we drew up outside the hotel, and my heart sank. It was one of the establishments from where coronavirus cases had helped start Victoria's huge second wave of cases, and its reputation wasn't pretty, even though the security contractors had clearly been delinquent and not the hotel.

"Look," I said, "the accommodation isn't really flash, and this is one of the places where the virus got away. The security people fucked up badly."

"We can't change it, can we?" Matt said. "Even Jamie Weiss couldn't interfere here."

"That's right. We have to remember these people are trying to keep us safe," I said, pointing to a tented area to one side of the driveway. "We get tested now, and also on the morning of day fourteen to ensure we're still negative."

The first surprise was the foyer, where everything appeared neat and clean. I suppose I expected dust sheets over the furniture, or similar, to indicate the gravity of the pandemic, but it appeared to be business as usual as Matt swiped our debit card. The only giveaway was the sheer number of security people present, most of whom seemed to be Middle Eastern. One made eye contact over his dark blue mask and seemed to take ownership of us once we'd checked in. He took our key and marched us toward the elevator and our home for the next two weeks on the twelfth floor. The rules in Melbourne seemed more flexible than in Hong Kong, where we couldn't leave the room except for urgent medical treatment. But now we were nearly home, we were adamant—we weren't going to be tempted by offers of exercise breaks outside or "special permits" for a variety of issues like mental health, etc. After our experiences in Thailand and Hong Kong, we wanted to stay put in our room. That way the risk of being reinfected was much reduced.

I glanced toward our security guard, then over at Matt, thinking, *I don't trust that guy.*

Matt smiled knowingly at me, on the same wavelength, as the guard unlocked our door. He handed Matt the key, his mouth agape as he caught sight of the one king bed in our room.

OUR ROOM was old but spotless, the linen worn and patched but freshly laundered before we arrived. A quarto sheet with the hotel's letterhead informed us the room had been "deep cleaned for your convenience and safety."

As we'd done in Hong Kong, we set up an exercise regime, which gave us some routine in the mornings. The hotel loaned us an old percolator, and we made our own coffee. It was surprisingly palatable, certainly better than the horrible instant rubbish which was part of the room package. We read the news online rather than take the faint risk of a virus-loaded newspaper. We spoke to all the family at separate times during the day by Face-Time and emailed with our friends in Thailand and Hong Kong. Meals were adequate without being brilliant, and time seldom dragged; boredom wasn't in our vocabulary.

I discovered there's nothing like a near-death experience to force you to appreciate the basics of life. Nothing. I was grateful to be alive, with my health improving every day, and both of us were happy to have this private time as a celebration and an opportunity. The confines of the room, we decided, felt more like a sanctuary than a jail, so isolation simply wasn't a problem. We didn't exhaust ourselves making love. I thought I'd have a lot to learn with limited male-on-male history, but Matt assured me I was fine the way I was. What he did, however, was to remind me there's a huge difference between having sex and making love—and how to be considerate of your partner's feelings, making sure there was mutual enjoyment of nature's gifts.

WE WERE relaxing on our first Saturday night in quarantine when the doorbell rasped, and I went to the peephole to inspect our visitor. It was Tarek, the guard who had escorted us to our room when we arrived. I cracked the door open on the security chain and he peered through the gap.

"Open up, open up," he said. "Room inspection."

"You must be joking," I told him.

"Open door immediately," Tarek insisted.

"Tarek, please leave," I said, "otherwise we will call security."

"I am security," he said, applying further pressure, and I looked at Matt for direction. Matt shook his head; we were miles ahead of Tarek, our mistrust of him justified.

"I think you like man," he said. "Open door."

"What would your wife say?" Matt asked, pointing to the band on his finger.

"She does as she told. Is not her business."

It was my turn, and I asked him to please keep his social distance because of COVID-19 concerns. He was already too close, the door straining on the security chain.

"Open door," he repeated.

"But this is why you are employed here," I said, "to stop the transmission of the disease. To keep people like ourselves from passing on the disease to other people, or vice versa."

"I think you'd better leave, mate," Matt said, quite kindly.

"No, I want fuck you both."

I closed the door in his face with some help from Matt, locking it from inside. Tarek would wake the entire hotel if he continued to argue, but after a few minutes it fell quiet again.

Early next morning there was a tap at the door, too soon for breakfast. I sprang out of bed and peered through the peephole. There was a very large woman standing there in security uniform, and I tentatively opened the door.

"Good morning," she said, "I am your new security person. Ursula is my name."

"Good morning," I said. "I'm Ben, and that's Matthew over there."

"I know. I look after you boys now. Please do not worry. If there is a problem, I fix."

We wondered what had happened to Tarek, but in fact we didn't see him again. Had the security management learned of his effort to get into our room? We never found out, but we were tested the day after his attempted incursion and were negative.

Our final week we wanted for nothing—our food improved from what was already quite acceptable, our laundry was free, and fresh sanitized fruit bowls changed daily. We were tested again on the fourteenth morning, given the all-clear at four o'clock that afternoon, and we breathed a sigh of relief. There was no waiting for our transfer; the government car rolled into the driveway a few minutes later and we were on our way home.

Matt appeared pensive, and I thought I knew why. "You were quiet the first time I brought you home because you didn't know what was ahead of you," I said. "You wondered if my family, now your family, would be any improvement on your birth family." He nodded, a smile on his lips, and I considered covering them with my own.

"Your family were amazing—funny, very loving, and enjoyed being bossed around when I took over the kitchen. For the first time in my life I experienced unconditional love, and I couldn't get enough." His smile faded, and he went on, "I wonder if they now realize I'm not a perfect person because I ran away from everyone, including you."

It suddenly occurred to me that my beautiful other half was having a needless crisis of confidence, which wouldn't be resolved in his mind until he made eye contact with our immediate family group—Mum, Jamie, who was now sharing the house with Mum, and Peter, our kid. Covid regulations specifically prevented visitors, so Tim and Kenny couldn't visit yet. Neither could Mia, Garry, and Erin, our little niece, born while we were in Hong Kong.

"No one's perfect," I responded. "If we were all perfect, life would be boring, and thank heavens you're not boring."

Matt laughed softly. He was never a giggler; when he laughed it was like a waterfall, smooth and continuous, so it was impossible not to be drawn to him. He slipped his seat belt and moved to the center belt position so we could cuddle. Our driver noticed in the rear-vision mirror, and I froze, knowing parts of our redneck society were still judgmental.

"Go for it, guys," he said with a smile. "It's lovely to see people being nice to each other for a change, not the opposite. Look out there." He pointed to the empty streets. "Inhospitable, unfriendly, and we're about to go into lockdown again with a curfew because of selfishness, ignorance, and plain stupidity. I didn't mean to listen in, but your obvious love of family and their concern for you guys is an inspiration. So good luck to you."

Chapter 59
HOME

IT WAS naturally an emotional occasion, all of us reacting to our own inner feelings. Guilt, fear, and uncertainty had all played a part, but within minutes we felt we'd never been away. I think our many telephone conversations over the previous two weeks had helped.

Social distancing here at home wasn't really necessary, but after a hug we kept apart, a sign of the times. Peter wasn't impressed; he hung over both of us, particularly Matt, indicating the bonding they shared had endured and looked even stronger. Already there were questions from Matt about his schooling, which was online these days, and if his room was clean, including the wardrobe where he normally "stored" things when cleaning the room.

"Oh no, it's perfect. I knew you'd have an inspection." Peter grinned, then dropped his head and burst into tears, his super IQ overtaken by feelings of being a normal little boy. "I didn't know if Dad was going to die and if you were going to forget about us," he wailed, and we circled him with our arms, rocking him like a baby until he calmed down. Mum and Jamie looked on, smiling at we three but not interrupting.

"So, Pete," Matt went on softly, "one of the reasons we're getting married is to ensure continuing stability in your life. You'll officially have two dads, and we'll share formal responsibility for you in a separate legal document, if that's okay." Peter didn't say anything, but his prodigious intelligence was obviously way ahead of us. "So we're not going anywhere without you, okay?" Matt kissed him on the cheek.

"But that's not the only reason you're getting married, is it?" Peter asked.

I knew Peter's insistence was fired by his curiosity, because he was my son, and I took up the cudgel. "No, it isn't. The other reason is that Matthew and I love each other, Pete. Even with all the shit we've been through and the hurt we've caused other people, both of us are old-fashioned. Australia is one of many countries that allows its same-sex couples to marry, and we think it's still the greatest compliment a couple can pay each other."

"Can I be a page boy?"

"No," I said. "I want you to give me away, to give my hand in marriage to Matt."

The expression on my child's face changed fleetingly from disappointment to delight as he absorbed the new information. "What do I have to do?" he asked.

"You have to stand by Dad's side," Matt said, "and when the celebrant asks, 'Who gives this man to be married?' you say 'I do.'"

"Cool, and who is giving you away?"

"My brother Will, but because of covid he won't be here. We'll have a video link so it will feel like he's here."

None of this was a surprise to anyone; Mum had helped us arrange a celebrant, who was due to do an online interview with us in the morning, and if she seemed okay, we'd have the papers delivered and signed tomorrow after lunch. Then we'd count forward a month or so and decide on a date. Our experiences in Hong Kong had simply solidified our desire to formalize our relationship quickly, both of us understanding that anything could happen to us in this new environment. We wanted to protect each other, and Peter in particular.

WE FELL into bed. While we'd only traveled from Melbourne today, we were emotionally exhausted, and we fell asleep after a kiss and a long cuddle where I was draped over Matt. I awoke in our own bed as the sun peeked weakly through the drapes, still feeling sleepy but at least rested. The space next to me was vacant, and I could vaguely hear him in the kitchen, already ordering people around, taking over the household again. I rolled out and had a wonderful pee in the en suite, and for once I thought I'd listen to my postcovid body and rest a bit more. A tap on the door proved to be Jamie, bearing a freshly made coffee from my old coffee machine, which only Matt had ever mastered.

"Your fiancé says you like your coffee like this. It looks like treacle."

"You have no appreciation of good coffee," I said, covering up my bareness as Jamie sat on the bed.

"How do you feel, mate?" he asked, looking at me through medically appraising eyes.

"I don't have all my strength back yet—that's why I seem to need my sleep—but I can smell and taste everything now, my appetite is good, and I'm feeling stronger each day."

"Breathing?"

"Improving. I reckon about eighty-five percent. No nasal discharge and only a tiny amount of congestion on the chest."

"You would have had X-rays. Any scarring on the lungs?"

"From what I remember, there was some slight damage, but according to Dr. Tang, it seemed to be healing, the damage reversing itself."

"Amazing. Your prognosis was so grave, we frankly didn't hold much hope for you, yet suddenly, in the space of a few hours, they woke you, nearly losing you on the way, and then, miraculously, you recovered with a smile on your face, asking for Matt."

I smiled at Jamie. "If I told you what I remember, you wouldn't believe me."

"Try me."

"Matt and I have always shared a closeness, even early in our friendship, but since we've become a couple, it seems to have intensified. It was Matt's voice that stopped me slipping away and brought me back from wherever I was headed. There's no doubt in my mind."

I thought Jamie, as an eminent physician, would scoff at my story, but his eyes were misty. "Yes, I do understand, mate. That's the power of love.

"As you may have gathered, your mother and I have become even closer through all of this, and we thought, if you approved, she might move into my house. It's sitting there doing nothing at the moment. We thought you guys needed some space to do your own thing, you know?"

"You dirty old man," I said. "Fancy doing horizontal lap dancing with my mother."

"Oh, what a little bitch you are," he snapped back.

"Takes one to know one."

"You taught me everything I know."

We laughed at each other. If anyone had overheard the conversation, they would have been puzzled; we sounded like social workers in a male bordello. But in fact it was Jamie and Ben reconnecting at our most outrageous.

"Um, there's some more news," Jamie said, peering at me closely. "We've had someone you know admitted to Waratah two weeks ago."

"Who?" I asked, mystified.

"Your father."

Chapter 60
DAD

HE WAS sitting in the corner of his room in a hospital chair, one of those designed for support and easier ingress and egress for frail patients. And he was certainly frail; his body was skin and bone, and his face, once handsome when he wasn't angry, was weatherbeaten and worn with deep creases. He still had all his hair, however. Thick as ever but now white as snow.

It was clear all the fight had gone out of him. He slumped in the chair in a gesture of capitulation.

"Hello, Dad," I said softly, and his head swept up, some interest in life returning.

He stared at me, crinkling his eyes. "Ben?" he asked, and I nodded.

"Yes, it's me, Dad. I came to say hello."

"What for? I treated you worse than anyone."

"Well, I work here part-time. I'm waiting for my nursing course to start up early next year, so with my own parent in here as a patient, I thought I'd better call around."

"Thanks, I don't deserve it."

"Why don't you deserve a visit?"

"Because I fucked up. I was pissed all the time, belted shit outta you kids and then yer mother. Then I drank all me assets, lost every bit of buildin' work I had, and I'm livin' on the disabled pension in a Housing Victoria shit box."

"Diddums."

"No need to make fuckin' fun of me."

"Dad, you're in your midfifties. You've got plenty of living to do if you only get your mind right."

"What's the use? My body's fucked completely."

"Not if you stay off the grog and have regular meals and exercise. You could live to a hundred."

"I don't want to, don't you get it? I don't have a single fucking thing to look forward to."

"All right, we'll agree to disagree," I said quietly, "but I got hooked on something a hundred times more addictive than alcohol, and I kicked it. I've been sober for nearly two years."

"Yeah, you tried to kill that fuckin' real-estate agent with your car. You needed a medal, not a jail sentence. What did they give you?"

"The bloke who runs this place—" I started to say, but Dad interrupted.

"Jamie Weiss. He's a good bloke, even though he's seeing your mother. He's a good man."

"Yes, well, thanks to him and Lewis Ferguson, I was sent to a place in Thailand after they dried me out here. And that's where I met my partner, and love did the rest. It's a long story."

I thought Dad would explode, but to my amazement it didn't happen; it appeared that old homophobic father of mine had sunk without trace.

"Your partner's a bloke, right?"

"Yes. His name's Matthew Wilson."

"You love him, right?"

"Yes."

"Then you're a lucky bloke. I'd like to meet him."

I THOUGHT Dad's attitude and remarks were amazing, given his previous history, but when I discussed it with Mum, she wasn't convinced that his changed behavior was permanent.

"Alcoholics get very cunning when they're recovering," she said. "They'll say anything to get them closer to their next drink. Very few in your father's age group stay dry for any length of time, and eventually they'll turn on you like a mad dog if they can't get what they want—another drink."

"I didn't turn on you when I hit the hooch."

"No, you didn't threaten me or the kids, or use violence of any sort. Quite the opposite—you always protected us."

"But I did some pretty awful stuff, Mum. I was affected by substance abuse like Dad, but people like you cared for me, and I escaped to live a relatively normal life. But I reckon Dad was an alcoholic before he even met you, and

I think he's had to hit rock bottom before he stopped drinking."

"And your point is, dear?"

"I reckon after you go to live with Jamie, we should bring him here to live. He won't last long living by himself."

"Ben, dear, I can never remember having an argument of any sort with you, and I don't want to start now. We've always been so close. However, if you bring your father here, the problem isn't his arrival in your life, it's when you have to get rid of him because he's causing trouble. That's the last thing Peter needs growing up—a nasty, argumentative old man who criticizes everything anyone does."

"Does Peter know of Dad's existence?" I asked.

"No, dear, all I did was to tell him the truth. How your father was an alcoholic, violent, and went to jail as a result. I told him I didn't know where he was, and that was the truth, until recently."

"It's sad that Peter's had you as his only grandparent. Tammy's parents have both passed away, I believe."

"Yes, I understand, Ben, but Jamie's been a good influence, and Kenny, Tim, Mia, and Garry have also spent a lot of time with him. I had the feeling that if you didn't survive in Hong Kong, Kenny and Tim would have tried to adopt him."

"They'd have to crawl over Matt to get to him, because Peter already knew he had two parents."

"That's where you've been blessed, Ben. I never had that love and trust. I had a demanding, drunken bully screaming at us all the time."

"Why did you marry him, Mum?"

"I was swept off my feet. He was so handsome, and believe it or not, he was a real gentleman until after we were married." Mum paused for a moment. There'd never been secrets between us, and I knew I was about to hear some very privileged information. "He was never a very intimate person, if you know what I mean, dear. It was almost like he was scared of intimacy, and I was raring to go." We both laughed, knowing we could share these snippets without them going anywhere else.

"I wonder if he was a closeted gay man," I said, almost to myself.

"That did occur to me, dear, because after Tim was born, there was nothing. It was like he'd done his duty and that was it."

"I hope Jamie's an improvement."

"He's wonderful. Always thinks of me before himself, like Matt's relationship with you."

I was happy to hear that. If anyone deserved the best, it was Mum.

Chapter 61
A NEW FAMILY DYNAMIC

SOMETIMES MIRACLES occur, and despite all the quarantine rules, Matt, Peter, and I were finally allowed to see my father together. I could come and go as I pleased because I worked at the Waratah Centre, but Matt and Peter had been forced to have covid testing, then quarantine at home for a few days to ensure a negative result.

Dad was a little brighter these days. I'd organized a podiatrist and insisted he spruce himself up a bit. A visiting barber had cut his hair neatly while I did some shopping for him. He was wearing some of the purchases—a new shirt and nice pants, not the bloody dreadful T-shirt and tracky pants which seem to be the uniform of all institutional inmates. I'd thrown out his smelly runners, and he had some leather casual shoes now that looked spiffy. All up he looked most presentable but still ten years older than his real age.

"Dad, this is Matthew, my fiancé, and our son and your grandson, Peter."

"My name's Frank, short for Francis John O'Connor," he said, standing up a little shakily but looking Matt in the eye. "I can't shake yer hand, because of this virus thing, but I do look forward to the day when I can. I don't like this bumping elbows rubbish. It looks like you've told a dirty joke and you're having a laugh about it."

Matt and Peter both laughed at the thought. My old man hadn't lost his Irish sense of humor, but I could tell Matt wanted to test the waters further.

"Well, I look forward to when Australian men get rid of their hang-ups and we can all have a lovely cuddle to say we care about each other."

"So do I," Dad said, and my mouth dropped open. "I wasted too much time worrying what other people thought rather than doing my own thing. When it's safe to get closer, I wanna be first in line to give you a cuddle, Matthew. You're not only a handsome bloke, but you've leg-roped my son, and from what I've heard, it wasn't an easy road you both traveled. I want to congratulate you on your engagement, and while I'm in no position to welcome you into the family, I'd like us to start a new branch of the family, even if I'm understandably not welcome over there."

"Yes, you are," Peter chipped in. "Gran will be all right. I have to talk to her."

Matt's eyes twinkled, and he winked at me. Peter was way ahead of us again; he'd heard enough from my father to make a judgment, and he simply expected Matt and me to follow his directions.

"Can I call you Pa?" Peter went on, "because I don't have a grandfather at all, and I think you would do a good job."

Dad's jaw dropped; I hadn't briefed him on Peter's IQ, and I could see the confusion in his eyes as he was confronted by a nearly ten-year-old boy with the intelligence of a twenty-five-year-old.

"Um, yes, of course," Dad said.

"That's excellent," Peter said, "because Dad isn't my birth father. He adopted me when my mother left us."

"Oh, I'm sorry to hear about your mother," Dad said, trying to be conciliatory.

"Oh, don't be. She left me with Dad because she knew Dad loved me and would be a better parent. But then I got extra lucky and got Matt as my other dad, so I'm really in the best possible place, aren't I?"

I thought my father would never close his mouth; like most people who met Peter for the first time, he was flabbergasted, such intelligence and perceptiveness so remarkable in someone so young.

"Yes, Peter," he said almost humbly, "I think you are in a good place, but you should know I wasn't a very nice man when I was younger, and I'm now paying the price for that behavior."

"You're a recovering alcoholic," said Peter, "and you must never have another drink or I'll do something terrible to you."

"No, Peter, I wouldn't dare."

"Good. We understand each other."

Dad looked at me, his eyes wide open in astonishment, but he didn't pursue the subject, I thought, out of respect (or even fear) of Peter. The two of them chatted away with no awkward silences—a lot of Irish jokes and all about Dad's life when he was Peter's age.

"What was your father like?" Peter asked.

"Oh, he was a terrible man," Dad said. "He regularly used a stock whip on me. I still have marks on my back all these years later."

My ears pricked up. I'd never heard any details of Dad's youth; his family in Limerick was never spoken about. My sole knowledge was that he and Mum met there when she was a tourist, married, and emigrated to Australia soon after.

"So what made your father do that to you?" Peter asked, and I thought Dad was about to cry, dropping his head into his hands.

"Old Grandpa, his father, was a cruel old man," Dad said, "a member of the IRA and so on. I don't want to give you nightmares at your tender age, so I'll save that story for another day. My father was in the pub every night, and so was I. We all drank to forget the nightmares of our country." Matt and I sat there, astonished, while Peter turned to us with pleading eyes. "The good thing is, Peter," Dad continued, "the cycle of male violence has finally stopped with your father."

"And with Uncle Tim," I said, and Dad nodded.

"Our family seems to have evolved to where its members live honestly. They live who they are, not what society demands they do," Dad said.

"They fall down every now and then, but they get up and get on with it."

I ORGANIZED some afternoon tea, Dad and Peter eating sandwiches and biscuits like it was their last meal. Peter then asked if he could be excused and left the room to find Jamie, understanding Matt and I needed some time alone with Dad.

"That was the first time I ever heard you speak of your life in Ireland," I said.

"It wan't pretty. That's why I never talked about it."

"Yet life in Ireland is quite different now," Matt said.

"Yes. To everyone's surprise, things like marriage equality happened, and my contacts tell me it is quite different now."

"How?" Matt asked.

"Well, these days if you get caught bad-mouthing a gay fella in public, yer can get fined—heavily. And if the wimmenfolk hear you doin' it, they turn off the supply, if yer know what I mean."

"So what you're saying, Frank, is that public opinion has changed massively," Matt said.

"Yes, same as Australia. You're a brave man now if you say anything bad about same-sex relations, although I'm told the really bad feelings in Limerick and Cork have gone underground. In Ireland forty-plus years ago, when I was growing up, if yer liked blokes, you were told to leave town or face the consequences. One couple was caught way back in the 1960s, before I was even born, and my grandfather was involved in their punishment."

"Punishment?"

"Yeah, the same as anyone caught passin' information to the British."

We gazed at Dad, and he sighed deeply, realizing we didn't have a clue what the "punishment" entailed.

"A deep trench got dug, usually in a plowed paddock, the accused was given a revolver, and they blew their brains out. If they were too slow, one of the boys does it for 'em. In this case they had a gun each and fired at the same time—end of story."

We grasped each other's hands, trying to cope with our mutual sense of horror. Matt recovered first and stared Dad down. "Why are you telling us this, Frank?" he asked.

"Because I cared for someone once, and my whole life might have changed if I'd dared to swim against the tide." Dad sighed and looked straight at me. "I needed you both to understand where I came from, the mental conditioning we all went through. It wasn't an option to disagree."

"But why tell us now? Why tell us at all, Dad?" I asked.

"Because this is the first time I've been sober since I was ten years old."

Chapter 62
NUPTIALS IN THE TIME OF CORONA

IT WAS our wedding day, the weak morning light peeking through the curtains as I rolled over to throw my arm around Matt and cuddle up. He mumbled something incoherent as I drifted back to sleep.

We woke again later to the sounds of activity in the lounge and realized the IT guys were setting up for the Zoom session that would connect our ceremony interstate and overseas. I was about to get up, but a hand grabbed me by a most important part of my anatomy, and a voice said, "Why don't you stay here for a while?" A grin spread across Matt's beautiful face. We'd been instructed by Mum, Jamie, and Peter that today, even in its modest form, was still our day, and we should relax and enjoy it. Matt sprang up, locked the door, and flew back to bed, and we began the day with our own celebration.

IN REGIONAL Victoria we were allowed ten people in the wedding party, including ourselves, the celebrant, and a witness each. Mum was to be my witness, and Jamie was Matt's choice, which brought us to five, plus Peter, Kenny, Tim, Mia, and Garry, with little Erin, who hopefully didn't count.

Importantly, the electronic hookup brought the outside world into the big lounge room at home. Dad would be connected via Zoom at Waratah, and Gloria, Phillip, and Amanda from her boardroom at Gloria Dixon Real Estate. Then there was Matt's brother Will and his wife and kids in Liverpool, New South Wales, the sole members of his own family group who remained supportive. At Jomtien, Ross, Yod and the resort staff would be watching, while Rama and Gavin would be online in Chiang Mai with their tiny son. In Hong Kong, Dr. Tang and her husband and son would be joining us, together with those who could be spared from the covid ward, and also Stephen Hoskings-Brown from the hotel—with his partner, Li.

I HOPED in this, my new life, that I'd learned something from my partner and soon-to-be husband. He was constantly assessing my feelings, asking how I felt about things and people, and importantly what made me happy, and also what made me sad—all part of our closeness as a couple. I decided on our wedding day to raise some issues that must have been uppermost in his mind right then. We finished our breakfast, and I led him into the garden. We sat on the old garden seat that he'd restored on his first visit here.

"It must be hard for you," I said. "You must have thoughts of your first wedding day and the ongoing aggression and disinterest of your own birth family, particularly after John died."

His face lit up, showing he understood why I was asking these questions at this time. "Yes and yes," he replied, "but I don't feel badly about either situation. John would have really liked you, Ben, and naturally I do reflect on the past. From time to time I feel him around, and the subliminal message, if there is one, is that he's delighted I've found happiness again. Don't forget it was you who finally pushed me to move on from his passing. You were so kind and loving when we met that first night in Jomtien.

"My birth family? Well, I actually feel sorry for them, because they're missing out on so much by being so insular. They've never moved far from home, and it's like life has passed them by. What's already happened is that even where they live, opinions on same-sex relations and marriage equality have changed so quickly and completely that their decision to disown me must make them feel like pariahs now."

"So you've actually forgiven them?"

"For want of a better expression, yes, I have, and in doing so, hopefully I've made myself and eventually our marriage stronger. There's nothing more damaging than trying to enter a new phase of your life with a chip on your shoulder. We should only be interested in positive thoughts and feelings, you and I, and expect those around us to be the same. Your family is now my family. I feel closer to them than I ever did to my birth family, with the exception of Will, of course."

I nodded in agreement as Peter called us inside. Coincidentally, it was the lovely Will, on the Zoom hookup nearly two hours early. Will and I had never met, but he was one of my favorite people. His support for Matt had never wavered. We'd spoken several times on FaceTime, but this was Zoom, and he looked nearly as handsome as his immediate brother. His wife, Sarah, was standing behind him, trying to restrain two tiny giggling little boys.

"Hey, lovebirds, how are ya?" he said. Before we had a chance to reply, he caught sight of me and whistled. "Hey, Benny boy, you look so good. You really well again, bro?"

"About ninety-five percent, and my lungs are nearly healed completely. Thanks, mate."

"Mate, you look so good I'd nearly jump the fence for ya."

We laughed at him. His off-the-cuff remark earned him a mild rebuke from his wife, who said with a straight face, "Jump the fence? You need to jump over the end of our own bed a bit more, thank you."

Will's face came into focus again, but this time he was more serious. "We just wanted some time with you before the wedding," he began.

I looked at Matt, who reached for my hand.

It was Sarah who spoke next. "My husband, as you know, Matt, is very sentimental. What he wants to say is that as you're formalizing a new family group, we'd love to be included. Will and Matt have parents with nothing to offer their grandchildren except hatred, and we want none of that. You guys will make wonderful uncles."

Chapter 63
I DO

FOOD WAS always important to the O'Connor clan, and Matt had strengthened our love of good wholesome home-cooked tucker. He'd even coached Mia in her culinary abilities, to the point where she insisted on providing a feast of finger food for the ceremony. Shortly after noon, it was served as a buffet, leaving us to enjoy each other's company. It was a late winter day and the weather was quite cool, about twelve degrees forecast, so the hot food was welcome. We'd only had a light breakfast, so I dived into the chili chicken wings in honey sauce, which were delicious, and fried garlic prawns on skewers, spicy rollmops, and mugs of steaming pumpkin soup full of chicken stock and olive oil.

Matt watched on, smiling and shaking his head as I went back for another serving of chicken wings, and I laughed. It was our wedding day after all, and Matt knew I had a personal celebration happening where I was at last feeling really well again. Our son also had a voracious appetite, but

Peter was a growing kid and burned the calories off instantly. He and I slipped around the corner, sharing a big plate of wings and prawns.

"Dad," he said, "you stink of garlic. You better clean your teeth, floss, and use mouthwash. You've gotta kiss Dad Matt soon."

We both ran to the en suite and cleaned our persons in the appropriate areas, then ran back to the others, giggling like two schoolgirls, or one schoolboy and an adult with an adolescent mindset.

Finally it was ceremony time, and we welcomed our guests from around Asia and Australia on Zoom as our celebrant began. We'd approved everything weeks prior, but hearing it again had an air of unreality for me. I'd been so antimarriage only a few years ago, and yet here I was, about to become part of that very institution, and I was loving it, because I'd fallen in love with an amazing person.

Edie, our celebrant and a friend of Mum's, was a retired schoolteacher in late middle age who believed marriage had to serve people, not the other way around, and she clearly had her own ideas as we formally joined our lives together.

"I know you would both like a no-fuss ceremony," she had said when we discussed how it would go, "but I wouldn't be doing my job if I didn't make your story, what makes you two unique as a couple, the centerpiece of your wedding."

We protested; we wanted a short, simple, and light-hearted event so we could fill what remained of the day with celebration, leaving the Zoom hookup intact for as long as possible. We didn't need or want the hearts and flowers, or the focus on us for too long. The sun would rise the following day with the duties that were important to us: educating Peter, me finishing my nursing degree, and the two of us generally caring for our family group, who had made so many sacrifices for us when we were in trouble. Matt would continue as a stay-at-home dad, and my father would move into the flat over the garage at home, with Mum's approval. Tim and Kenny were pursuing surrogacy, and Mia was again preggers, which was wonderful.

But Edie was adamant. "Your story is important," she said. "Young people growing up in the new generations will hear about it and understand the power of love, how it can transform lives. I want to deliver a ceremony full of dignity, pathos, the triumph of good over evil, and what a positive effect you two will have on the future of young couples in this town."

We capitulated. Edie read back the ceremony, and we corrected a few mistakes, so at least we knew what was coming at us.

As the ceremony began, I looked over the bank of monitors at our friends watching and reached for Matthew's hand.

"No one's smiling," I whispered. "They all look so serious."

Edie glared at me, her schoolmarm persona taking over. I imagined being sent out of the room and given a good caning for my disrespect. Matt squeezed my hand as Edie went into launch mode with stentorian tonality, a commanding presence in her academic gown, complete with a fucking mortarboard.

She told our story up front. How we had had a "oneness" where we were so close we could literally read each other's minds from time to time—how it was even a part of my recovery from covid. She slipped back in time, reminding everyone where we'd come from in our previous lives and how love saved us from an aimless, drug-fueled existence that had no future and no joy.

I looked at Dad on his screen. He looked so miserable, and I felt for him and his ruined life. Now he'd stopped drinking, maybe he could find some happiness again.

Eddie Chan suddenly came online from the hospital, and I waved to him as he apologized for his lateness. He'd been called in for an emergency. He and Dr. Tang had a quick conversation, during which Edie seemed about to explode.

Then I heard Gloria's booming voice from her boardroom, apologizing because another two guests had walked in—my amazing solicitor, Lewis Ferguson, and his husband, Ted, out of quarantine after their South American holiday, rescued by a government flight. We didn't think they'd be there, but they were. Lewis, Jamie, and Mum exchanged some lovely insults with each other, as if time had stood still.

Some things never change, I thought, as Edie cleared her voice, preparing to resume, her face a ruddy puce color.

"Now," she thundered, "who gives this man, Benjamin John O'Connor, in marriage?"

Our clever little boy, with a smug look on his face, turned toward Dad's monitor. "You ready, Pa?" he said. "On the count of three.... We do," they said together in perfect synchrony. We watched Mum's face, which was a study of pride, not animosity. I wondered in fact if she'd helped organize it.

"Of course," Matt whispered. He knew exactly what I was thinking.

"And," roared Edie, "who gives this man, Matthew Wilson, in marriage?"

"We do" came the loud reply, and it was obvious Will, Sarah, and their little boys had also been rehearsing.

Matt smiled and thanked them; then a tear escaped his right eye, and I kissed it better. It had the desired effect and loosened up our audience but nearly set Edie right off. The mortarboard wobbled, and I had a vision of our Edie throwing the fucking thing at the very next person who interrupted.

Then she read the Monitum like she was addressing year twelve students, filling them with fear and foreboding if they strayed from the straight and narrow in the future. It was intended as a rebuke from Australia, explaining what the country thought marriage should be all about, and Edie clearly loved putting us back in our little boxes where she thought we belonged. Then there was a thing called the Asking, where we confirmed she was on the right track, that indeed we did want to marry each other. And then came the Vows, which we knew were the most legal part of the ceremony. We repeated them one line at a time, very formal and very precise. I studied the monitors and saw morose expressions everywhere from sheer boredom, where there should have been joy and laughter. I was glad the formalities were nearly over.

Finally, after exchanging rings, it was the Declaration, where Edie announced, in loud, perfectly enunciated words, "It has been my honor to officiate at your ceremony today. On behalf of the people of Australia, your family and friends, I declare that you, Benjamin John O'Connor, and you, Matthew Wilson, are now husbands together. Congratulations, you may now each kiss your husband."

I turned toward him, and he grinned at me as I leaned in deeply—and farted.

It wasn't a quiet one, either. It was a full-throated roar that could no doubt be heard on the other side of town. Mia's garlic prawns had done more than Edie could have; they made everyone laugh. The monitors erupted in mirth.

"Thunder Downunder," shouted Ross.

Dr. Tang gave me the most beautiful smile. As the laughter quietened down, she leaned into the camera. "Mr. Ben, you are very well, I think. Your digestive system working beautifully. Keep up the good work—eat plenty, stay healthy."

It wasn't just the noise of the rushing air, either. An all-pervasive odor crept up on us, and Mum groaned, pointing upward. "Peter," she said, "the overhead fans."

Pete grinned. The switch was on the wall near where he was sitting, and as he turned in his chair, he reached up and delivered another depth charge to the gathering, even louder than mine, and judging by the reaction of those nearest, smelling even worse.

Edie tried to be all serous and scholarly, but even she had to laugh as we all fell about.

"Having a good day over there?" roared Gloria.

"Oh, we're having a real shit of a day," Matt said, the tears running down his face.

We sat down finally and signed the documents, and Edie presented the Certificate of Marriage. She told us later, as she was poured into a taxi, she'd never realized how laughter cured just about everything and how clever she'd felt after her twelfth glass of red.

We both noticed Mum and Jamie talking to Dad via his monitor and marveled how the adults had grown up around us. Happily, in Liverpool, Will's family had also become our family.

I turned to my new husband, who'd been with me through thick and thin, sickness and health, joy and celebration. "Coming to bed, Isabella?"

"Thought you'd never ask, Ferdinand."

JOHN TERRY MOORE hails originally from Tasmania, the Australian island state. He completed his education at Hobart Matriculation College, was a farmer and Tasmanian champion single sculler for several years, runner-up in the Australian competition.

After coming out to his family, John made his home in Victoria, holding a number of senior positions in the Victorian automotive industry over a thirty-five-year period. Subsequently, he became a civil marriage and funeral celebrant for many years (now retired), witnessing firsthand rapidly changing Australian public opinion, questioning traditional family structures and culminating in the marriage equality legislation passing into law in December 2017. However, John remains concerned that the fight is never over; right wing politicians, together with some church leaders would seek to wind back the clock to the bad old days where the scourge of homophobia was a major cause of suicide in men under thirty years of age.

Consequently, John seeks to normalize same-sex relationships and inclusiveness through his writing, encouraging all young people to live their lives truthfully, fearlessly, and with dignity, as is their right.

John's interest in economics, politics, and Asian affairs has also played a major role in his writing, and he is unfazed in taking on contemporary issues such as drug use, particularly the unpredictable nature of methamphetamines, and the scourge of coronavirus.

John and his husband have traveled extensively throughout Asia, inserting themselves into the culture and the daily lifestyles of the local people, and consequently have a unique overview and a deep understanding of Asian and South Asian nations, which also feature in his writing.

John and his husband, Russell Baum, live in Geelong, Victoria's largest regional center, one hour from Melbourne, Australia. They were flower growers, raised stud sheep, and bred Kelpies, Australia's working dogs, before moving to Wandana Heights, a Geelong suburb, in semiretirement.

There they have a large network of friends, mostly with canine interests in common. John collects clocks when time permits and fervently espouses the health benefits of red wine.

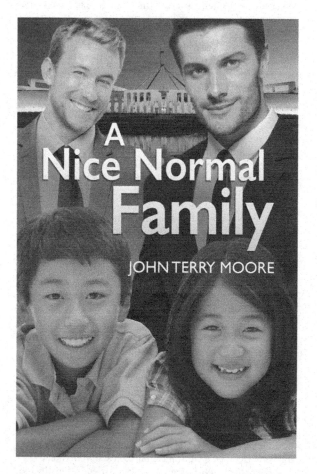

A
Nice Normal
Family

JOHN TERRY MOORE

Jackson "Jacko" Smith is dyslexic, but like many people affected by the learning disability, he is highly intelligent. His best friend Sammy Collins helps him get through school and unlocks his potential. Jacko progresses through the ranks of local government until Mother Nature intervenes and the straight boy and the gay boy become a couple.

As Jacko and Sammy start a family and challenge social mores, Jacko enters politics, horrified at the direction the Australian government is taking. With Sammy by his side, he can achieve anything and rises through the ranks to the highest office in the land, driving Australia away from its British colonial roots and engaging with its neighbors in Asia like never before. Economic growth results, and while most Australians are supportive, a small group of extremists might endanger everything Jacko has built—including his life.

Through the love and the strength of their partnership, Jacko and Sammy rise above their ordinary lives. Because love is never ordinary.

www.dreamspinnerpress.com